The Cowboy Collection

KISSED BY A COWBOY
SEALED WITH A KISS
MISTLETOE COWBOY

LACY WILLIAMS

DEDICATION

To Luke, who is not a cowboy but always my hero.

KISSED BY A COWBOY

PROLOGUE

Prom night – twelve years ago.

This was a mistake.

The words reverberated through seventeen-year-old Haley Carston's head. Pulsed painfully through her heart.

They even trembled in her hands.

The pale pink princess-style prom dress poufed around her. There was no other word to describe it other than *poufed*. She looked like a strawberry cupcake.

The girl staring back at her in Katie's full-length mirror looked like a stranger. Too much blush, too much mascara. Dark pink lipstick. How had she let her new friend talk her into this much makeup?

Because everyone *let* Katie. Katie was that kind of person. The shining star.

Nothing like *tag-along Haley*.

But that girl in the mirror—she was a stranger.

Except for the scared eyes. Those were all Haley.

After Katie had found out she wasn't planning to go to the senior prom, she'd promised to find Haley a date. And no one said no to Katie.

But who could she have found?

Haley's dad had dragged her to Redbud Trails, Oklahoma in the middle of her senior year, after a job he'd been chasing hadn't panned out. They'd planned to leave after a few weeks, but Haley's Aunt Matilda had seen how unhappy she was at the prospect of moving again and offered to let her stay until her first semester of college.

Haley had expected to hate the minuscule high school, graduating class of a whole dozen. She'd never imagined she'd fit in, figuring she'd stick out like the outsider she was.

Instead, she'd found an immediate friend in Katie, who'd taken Haley under her wing and drawn her into her circle of friends—the popular kids—and made Haley forget that she hadn't been born and raised in small-town Oklahoma.

Most of the time.

Tonight, she felt like a silk flower in a room full of hothouse roses. Pretending she was one of the crowd but woefully inadequate.

The three-inch pumps that matched the dress were already pinching her toes. She wobbled into the hallway and hesitated outside Katie's bedroom doorway. How in the world was she going to get to the first floor without tumbling down them?

"What are we waiting for?" Haley recognized the complaining male voice wafting up from the living room—Katie's boyfriend-of-the-month, Ronald Walker. Katie had commented more than once about how fine they would look in their prom pictures together. Haley thought maybe that was the only reason her friend was dating the jock and half-expected a breakup soon after tonight.

"Haley will be down in a minute," Katie said.

Showtime.

There were other voices laughing and talking. Katie had convinced the group to meet up at the Michaels' farm and carpool. Which meant more people to see Haley descend and face whatever sap Katie had found for her, some guy who felt sorry enough for Haley to be her date.

Her feet didn't want to move. But she was afraid Katie would come upstairs looking for her if she didn't go. She took the first step and let her momentum carry her down, down...

Voices got louder. It sounded like Katie had a crowd of friends in the living room.

"Maddox, heads up!"

When she heard the name, Haley lifted her gaze from the stairs, and she stumbled on the last step. She barely registered the projectile flying toward her until it *whacked* the back of her shoulder. Her foot caught in the long dress, and she tilted precariously.

A strong pair of hands caught her waist and steadied her.

And a kid-sized play football fell to the floor.

"Sorry," Katie's younger brother Justin, a freshman, muttered from somewhere off to the side.

Haley looked up . . . and up . . . and up into the strong-jawed face of Maddox Michaels, Katie's older brother.

Who should've been in jeans and a Stetson but instead was wearing a smart black suit and white shirt and black tie...

No. Oh no.

"Great, we're all here!" Katie sang out. "Let's have mom do her three hundred pictures so we can go."

Maddox let go of Haley's waist, but only after he made sure she was steady in the uncomfortable heels. "All right?" he asked easily.

She nodded dumbly, her cheeks burning hotter than the face of the sun. She'd only met Maddox twice before, and she'd found herself tongue-tied both times.

He was *handsome*. A *college guy*.

And she couldn't even stutter out a sentence!

"I think this belongs to you." He presented her with a simple wrist corsage of white roses. His fingers were hot on her wrist as he slipped it over her hand.

"Oh, um..." *Thank you.* How hard would that have been to say? But she only had one thought blaring through her brain. *Find Katie!*

She excused herself—had she even said *pardon me?*—and moved faster than the shoes should have allowed, pushing through the other bodies crowding the room. There Katie was, coming out of the kitchen. Haley took her friend's arm and ducked back into the brightly-lit room.

"I can't go to *prom* with *your brother*," she hissed.

Katie patted her hand, looking over Haley's shoulder back into the other room. "Look, I know he's an old curmudgeon..."

Curmudgeon? Was Katie insane? Her brother was...was

amazing. Sure, he occasionally got irritated with Katie's wild schemes, but then, who wouldn't?

He'd just finished his freshman year on a football scholarship—quarterback, no less. And there was talk that a Division I team wanted to recruit him. He was that good.

And that far out of her league. What would she even say to him? Had Katie lost her ever-lovin' mind?

Katie's smile turned apologetic. "But he was the only one..." ...*who would go with you.*

Her friend didn't have the finish the sentence. The words Katie didn't say hurt just the same.

"Look, I don't have to go to prom," Haley whispered frantically. "I can just go home, and then he won't have to pretend to be my date."

"Quit worrying." Katie waved her hand like she was brushing away a gnat. "Everything will be fine. Everyone will be so focused on him, they won't even notice you."

Great.

And Katie was right.

Against her better judgment, Haley squeezed into the suburban Ronald had borrowed from his mom. She would've pressed up against the window but her voluminous skirt prevented her from scooting far enough in. Her face burned as Maddox calmly settled his lanky body beside her, one long leg pressing into the pink layers.

His shoulders were so wide he had to rest his arm behind her on the seat.

It took all her energy to keep from falling into him as Ronald showed off for the guys, speeding around corners until Haley thought she might get carsick. By the time they got to the banquet hall, her whole body ached from tension, and she hadn't danced a single song yet.

Maddox helped her out of the vehicle, and within seconds, they found themselves surrounded by guys offering high-fives and talking about the last games of the season. Girls flirted with him as if Haley weren't even there.

She couldn't believe Katie had done this to her.

#

Maddox wanted to kill his sister.

Not for the date. He'd met Haley a couple times before, and she seemed all right. Maybe a little shy, but not starstruck like a lot of the other high school kids.

Tonight was supposed to be three or four hours hanging out with Haley and his sister's friends. Home by midnight. No big deal.

But he hadn't counted on the other kids. They followed him around all night until he felt like a celebrity trying to avoid the paparazzi.

About halfway through the evening, he finally spotted a patch of daylight in the crowd and broke into the open field. Out of the decorated banquet room. All the way outside. There was a little church next door with a small playground and he made a beeline for it like he had a linebacker on his tail.

He probably shouldn't have pulled his date out with him. It had been sheer reflex to grab her hand when he'd made his escape.

But now that they were alone, he had second thoughts and dropped her hand. Maybe he should've left her in there with her friends. She was so quiet—it made her seem more mature or something—he kept forgetting she was a year younger than him.

The cool night air felt good against his hot face, but he still couldn't breathe. He loosened his tie, sticking a finger down his collar to try and alleviate the choking sensation.

Everyone's expectations were stifling. Even his mother! He remembered her whispered words before he'd left the house that night. *"Just don't get her pregnant—you don't want to ruin your life."* How embarrassing, and really, did his own mother not know him better than that? And what about ruining *Haley's life*? His mom didn't seem to have spared a thought for Haley at all.

He should be used to the pressure. After his dad drank himself to death when Maddox had been fourteen, she'd started calling him *man of the house*. He'd worked early mornings before practice and into the night, keeping the farm out of bankruptcy after his dad had almost lost it all.

And now that there was a hint of fame on the horizon, his mom had become obsessed with Maddox's football career.

The expectations wore on him.

Football season didn't start for months, but he already felt like he was about to be blitzed.

Even so, he should probably suck it up and be sociable for another hour or so, until they could get out of here. He looked up.

It was full dark out, but an outside light on the corner of the building illuminated Haley. She was watching him, her lower lip caught between her teeth.

"Sorry," he said.

She folded her arms around her middle and shrugged. Her dress was pretty, but she seemed uncomfortable. With him, or with the situation?

He nodded toward the banquet hall they'd come from. "I didn't realize it was going to turn into such a zoo."

She shrugged again. She was so *quiet*, he couldn't get a read on her.

"You're not having fun," he guessed. He turned slightly away and ran a hand through his hair. "This was a bad idea." He gave the empty merry-go-round a shove, sending it spinning. "This is probably a nightmare compared to how you imagined your senior prom."

"I never imagined it," she whispered.

He barely heard her over the metal squeaking as the merry-go-round wound down.

"Why not?" He glanced back at her.

She looked into the distance, still clutching her elbows with both hands. "My dad and I move around a lot. This is my fifth school in three years."

"So...?"

"So it's hard for me to make friends. I never planned on *going* to senior prom, but Katie..."

"Katie," he agreed, trying for lighthearted.

Instead of smiling, she turned her face to the side. "Sorry

you got stuck with me," she muttered.

"I'm not." He probably surprised them both with the statement. "Unlike most everybody else, I know how to say *no* to Katie."

In the dim light he could see her luminous hazel eyes. Maybe they were filled with hope, with expectations, but somehow, she didn't make his chest tighten up like all the other kids did.

"We didn't get to dance," he said. When he reached for her, she stepped into his arms. He'd expected her to be hesitant, and maybe she was, but somehow, she fit there, in his arms. His heart pounded like he was about to throw a fourth and goal. He shuffled his feet, barely moving to the muffled notes audible even though they were outdoors and away from the dance.

What was going on here?

"I'm sorry about all of...them," he finished lamely. All the fanfare, the kids following him around all night. They'd all heard about State sniffing around after the season wrapped. If he was recruited, there was a chance he'd been seen by the pro scouts.

His mother, his friends—heck, the whole town had stars in their eyes.

"I don't think they get it," she said softly, her words a puff of warmth against his neck. "Only like one percent of all college players get drafted to the NFL."

She peered up at him, biting her lip again like maybe she shouldn't have said that.

"You're a football fan?"

"Not really. My dad."

He was having a hard time concentrating on talking. He didn't want to think about all those *expectations*. Not right now.

She said softly, "It's a lot of hard work."

Looking down on her, he thought about the kind of work it would take to get to know someone like Haley. She wasn't the typical girl, falling all over herself to get him to like her. She was...real, somehow.

"I'm not afraid of hard work."

He saw goosebumps rise along the slope of her shoulders, felt her shiver through his hands at her waist.

"Do you have a backup plan?" she asked. "In case the football thing doesn't pan out?"

Here was another reason to like Haley. Her smarts. Once, he'd overheard her coaching Katie before a big test. Now that he knew she had moved from school to school, it was even more impressive that she could keep up with the assigned work.

He pulled her to his chest, and her face tipped up to his.

He thought he should probably kiss her.

When their lips were only an inch apart, she leaned back. "I don't want you to kiss me, just because Katie forced you to be my date."

And that's the moment he fell a little bit in love with Haley Carston.

"All right."

And he bent his head to kiss her anyway.

CHAPTER ONE

Present day.
Haley Carston walked out of the bank and into the mid-June day. Summer was coming to western Oklahoma, and she knew better than to expect this mild weather to last.

She clutched the manila folder in one hand. The power of attorney for her aunt was a sign that everything was changing—and Haley didn't want it to. But she didn't get a choice. Life was like that sometimes—which she knew better than anyone.

The gilded glass door locked behind her with a decisive click. Haley had been the last customer of the day, and her business had taken longer than she'd wanted. No doubt the bank employees were in a rush to get home.

It shouldn't have taken nearly so long, but several of the employees had wandered into the bank manager's office to greet her like the old friend that she wasn't.

She'd only been back in Redbud Trails, Oklahoma, for a week, but the small town seemed to have a long memory. Everyone remembered her as *Katie Michaels' tag-along,* even though it had been over a decade since she'd left for college and stayed in Oklahoma City. She'd already lost count of the times she'd heard someone say, *"You used to run around with the Michaels girl."*

She squinted in the afternoon sunlight. Her memories of Katie were like a giant fist squeezing her insides and twisting. Haley had worked hard during college to shed the perpetual shyness that had followed her to the state university. But she'd never forgotten her best friend. Katie was a light that had shone too brightly—and burned out too quickly.

Just like Aunt Matilda. Haley's aunt had been diagnosed with inoperable cancer and wouldn't last the summer. One thing Haley had learned from growing up the way she had was you didn't get that time back. Her boss had granted her a leave of absence, and she arrived in Redbud Trails the next day.

Aunt Matilda needed her. And her aunt had been there for Haley through the dark days after Paul had walked away. Haley would stay by her aunt's side until the end.

Even if it was hard.

She paused to take a breath and admire the picturesque square in front of the bank. It had always been her favorite place in this own. Just as she was turning away, a small voice cried out, "Wait!"

A young girl rode up on a bicycle, dark pigtails flying out behind her, red-faced and huffing, her forehead slick with sweat. She hopped off the bike before it had even stopped rolling. She didn't even glance at Haley but ran up to the glass door and banged on it. Her purple backpack bounced with the force of her whacking.

"Please—" the girl gasped. She sounded near tears.

And the bank was most definitely closed.

"Honey," Haley said, "I don't think they're going to open for you."

The girl just banged harder. Stubborn.

"They c-can't be closed. I need to talk to a loan officer. I have to show them!"

What was the girl so upset about? Haley looked for a parent, figuring that *someone* must be responsible for her. The girl looked about ten, but that was still too young to be in town, alone.

But no one was around.

"Hey." Haley approached the girl and put her hand on her shoulder.

The insistent banging finally stopped. The girl's head and shoulders drooped. She sniffled and rubbed a hand beneath her eyes, still looking down.

"Can I help you, hon?" Haley asked.

The little girl looked up, giving Haley her first good look at the turned-up tip of her nose, splash of freckles, and blue eyes. Her heart nearly stopped. The girl was a near-carbon copy of Katie. Down to the thick, curling eyelashes that Haley had been so jealous of back then.

She might've been the image of her mother, but the hesitant wariness in her gaze was all her Uncle Maddox. Haley's insides dipped at the single thought of the man she hadn't seen in over a decade.

"You're Livy, right? Livy Michaels?" Haley asked. "I'm Haley Carston."

The girl didn't react to Haley's name. Haley had rarely visited Redbud Trails after she'd entered college. Aunt Matilda had mostly opted to come down to the city. And Haley doubted Livy's uncle had ever mentioned her.

"Nobody calls me that," the girl said, pulling away and crossing her arms.

"Oh. Sorry. Olivia." Haley smiled, trying to show that she was a friend. She'd heard Katie call her the nickname once, right after Olivia had been born. Maybe the pet name hadn't stuck. Because Katie hadn't been around to use it.

"You look like your mother."

The softly-spoken statement did not gain Haley any points with Olivia, who watched her with slightly-narrowed eyes.

And there was still no parental figure in sight. "Is your uncle...?"

Olivia's expression changed to slightly-chagrined. "Um... I told Uncle Justin I was riding my bike."

To town? Haley's suspicions rose. She knew Maddox's mother had passed and had heard Maddox had custody of the little girl. Maybe Justin was watching her this afternoon.

"I really need to talk to a banker," Olivia said again, voice gone tiny. "It's important."

No one had even come to the door to see what all the banging was about. If Haley had to guess, the bank tellers and manager might've already left by a back exit.

"I don't think that's going to happen tonight. What about your uncle?"

Olivia looked away. "He's...um...he's on his way."

A likely story. "Can I give you a ride somewhere? Or walk with you...?"

Olivia's face scrunched. "I'm not supposed to ride with people I don't know."

Haley bit the inside of her lip, thinking. She couldn't just leave an eleven-year-old alone here, not knowing when one of Olivia's uncles might appear.

"Hmm. Well, you might not know me, but you probably know my aunt. Matilda Patterson."

The girl's face brightened. "Everyone knows Mrs. Matilda."

It was so bittersweet. Not many knew about her aunt's illness, and Haley's voice was soft when she answered the girl. "I know Aunt Matilda would love to see you. We can call your uncle and make sure it's all right. He can pick you up there."

The tip of Olivia's ears went pink. She turned her face to the ground.

Haley hated to be the bad guy but, "He's probably worried sick. I assume he has a cell phone...?" She fished her phone out of her purse and waited for Olivia to give her the number.

"Honey?"

Finally, Olivia rattled off a number, but when a gruff male voice answered with a curt, "Yeah?" Haley's heart pounded in her throat and ears.

The man on the line wasn't Justin.

It was Maddox.

"M-Maddox?" Oh, Haley hated the stutter that slipped into her voice.

There was a pause. Then a gruff, "Who is this?"

Looking up with an expression so like her mother's, Olivia's lower lip stuck out the slightest bit, her eyes pleading for Haley's understanding. Or help. How many times had Katie used that very look on Haley?

And apparently, it still worked.

Haley forced a polite, cheerful note into her voice, the same note she reserved for her coworkers back in Oklahoma City. "This is Haley Carston."

She didn't exactly expect a warm welcome, maybe more of a *what do you want*, given how they'd left things, but he was completely silent. She could hear the rumble of an engine, muffled like he was in the cab of a truck. Maybe he really was on his way.

"I'm in town for awhile, and I ran into your niece outside the Redbud Trails Bank. I wanted to see if she could come over to Aunt Matilda's with me until you or Justin can come pick her up."

"She's in town? Alone?" he barked. And she recognized the worry beneath the gruffness.

Olivia watched, clutching her hands together in front of her.

"Mmhmm," Haley said, her tone unnaturally bright.

He muttered under his breath. She thought it might've been something derogatory toward his brother, but she couldn't be sure.

"Justin can't drive," he said. "And I'm on my way home, but I'm probably an hour out of town."

"Well, Aunt Matilda and I would love to have Olivia over," Haley said.

He hesitated. "Are you sure?"

"Of course."

"I'll be there as soon as I can."

Maddox Michaels stood on the porch of the little Patterson cottage and braced his hand on the doorframe, letting his head hang low.

One of the large dining room windows was open a few inches, and he could hear Olivia chattering from somewhere in the house. Relief swamped him. She was okay.

He was going to kill his brother. Justin was supposed to have been *watching* her.

It was probably an act of mercy that Haley had found his

niece. Maddox was working for a custom harvester, trading shifts with another guy who had a new baby at home. The crew would travel all summer, running combines and a grain cart. Dave needed the extra income but didn't want to miss time with his new baby, and with Justin incapacitated, Maddox needed to be home more, too. Right now, they were working in southern Oklahoma, but they would also travel up through Kansas and Colorado and who knew where else. Maddox didn't like the travel, but he needed the money, and splitting the time on the crew seemed to be working for both of them.

Until now.

Coming face-to-face with Haley was the last thing he wanted to do when he was feeling exhausted and beat-down. How in the world had Olivia gotten to town?

In his peripheral vision, he caught sight of the dusty pink bike leaning against the front of the truck parked beneath the carport, and the muscles in his neck and shoulders tightened. His hand slipped down the doorframe.

No. Olivia wouldn't have ridden her bike into town alone. It was three and a quarter miles to the bank.

Justin was a dead man.

The door opened before he was ready, and he looked up. Slowly. His Stetson moved with his head, revealing her inch-by-inch.

But it didn't soften the blow of seeing her.

Her feet were bare beneath hip-hugging jeans, and she wore some kind of soft, flowy blouse. Her auburn hair was shorter, curling around her face.

And her brown eyes were as soft as he remembered.

She reached out and touched his forearm, and that's when he realized he'd leaned his palm against the doorbell. The buzzer had been sounding consistently. Annoyingly.

"Sorry."

"It's okay," she said. "Hi."

"Hi."

She was the same as she had been. That smile. Half shy and half knowing, and his gut twisted like he was nineteen again.

"You look good," she said softly.

He knew what he looked like. Older. Worry creases around his eyes. Covered in dust and wrinkled, like he'd slept in his truck. Which he had.

"You too." It was such an inane comment, and *good* didn't even come close to describing her. He needed to get out of here before he made more of a fool of himself.

"Can you send Olivia out? Is she okay?"

Haley's expression softened. "She's amazing. She's helping me cook supper. C'mon in."

He shouldn't. She must've seen his hesitation, because she paused on the threshold. "If you want to stay, Matilda and I would love to have you for supper. Either way, there's something I'd like to talk to you about."

He nodded. He swung his tired body into motion and stepped inside. Ahead and off to the left was the quaint, antiquey living room.

"Are you limping?" she asked.

He took off his hat, ran a hand through his brown curls, damp from sweating beneath the hat brim. The A/C on his pickup wasn't the best, but there was no money to fix it right now.

"Just tired. I've been out of town." His joints had gotten stiff sitting in his truck for hours. "I've picked up a job working with a harvest crew."

"Oh. So you have to travel a lot?"

"Yeah, a few days at a time. The farm's doing good though." If he could just keep ahead of his creditors. "Since Katie and my mom passed, it's just been me, Justin, and Olivia."

He tapped his hat against his leg. Nervous. And rambling. But seeing her again, after all this time... all his feelings came rushing back, like they'd been jostled loose by the vibrations of the combine.

He rubbed the back of his neck as he followed her through the dining room, where papers were strewn across the worn, wooden table. Past the dining room, he could see into a small kitchen.

That last summer, after Haley's senior prom, he'd followed Katie and Haley around like a safety chasing a wide receiver. He'd tried to be nonchalant about it, just show up wherever they were. He was pretty sure Katie had seen through him, but he didn't know if Haley had ever figured out how he felt about her.

And then Katie's pregnancy changed everything. Derailed his plans.

And heaped on another responsibility. Not that he regretted having charge of Olivia, but he'd only been twenty-one.

And speaking of.

"I should check on..." He nodded to the kitchen.

He passed by Haley, getting a whiff of something flowery.

Olivia caught sight of him and sent him a chagrined smile, not letting go of the spoon she held in one hand. "Hey, Uncle M."

Her subdued greeting was not lost on him, nothing like the chattering he'd heard before, through the open window.

She was safe. Thank God. He swallowed the emotion that tightened his throat. "You're in trouble, you know that?"

"I'm sorry," Olivia whispered.

"What exactly were you thinking?"

"I needed to go to the bank."

He shook his head, didn't even know what to say. What she'd done was dangerous. Then he got a whiff and a glimpse of the pan she was tending. "What is that?"

She said something he didn't understand, her voice still soft and subdued.

"What?" he asked warily.

"Duck," answered Haley. "It's French."

He wasn't sure what to think about that, and it must've shown in his face, because Olivia giggled hesitantly.

"Uncle M is more of a steak and potatoes kind of guy," his niece offered.

He shrugged. It was true.

"Well, maybe it's a good thing you and I met," Haley told Olivia. "We can both appreciate the finer culinary arts."

He watched Olivia repeatedly scoop up the sauce in the pan and drizzle it over the duck. He'd never seen her do anything like that before. "Where did you learn to do that?"

"Food Network," Olivia said at the same time that Haley said, "Cooking classes."

The girls shared a smile, and the sight of it was like getting socked in the solar plexus. How long had it been since Olivia had smiled at him like that? How had his niece formed a connection with Haley in just an hour? Was it the cooking together? Or was it because they were both female?

He didn't know, and he wasn't sure he wanted to find out. "We've gotta head home, kid."

Olivia and Haley shared a glance, and he braced himself for the upcoming battle.

But it wasn't Olivia who begged him to stay.

"I know you've got places to be," Haley said. "But I want to talk to you for a minute."

This was a little surreal.

Haley couldn't believe that Maddox was really here. The first man who'd kissed her.

The man she'd dreamed would fall in love with her and want to marry her. At least she'd dreamed it until Katie's death had changed everything.

He followed her back into the dining room. She stepped on one side of the table and turned to see he'd paused on the opposite side. He faced her like she was the opposing team. His broad shoulders—football shoulders—filled out the plain blue t-shirt, and his hair clung to his head after being under his cowboy hat all day.

But it was the shadows in his coffee-colored eyes that had her breath catching in her chest. This wasn't the confident *all of life ahead of him* Maddox that she remembered so vividly from that summer.

"Where's Matilda?" he asked with a glance toward the living

room.

Tears rose in the back of her throat, but she coughed them away. "Napping," she said.

His eyes questioned her, and she shook her head. "She's been diagnosed with...cancer." The word was a knife in her throat. "The doctors say..." She took a breath. And still couldn't say it. "So I'm here."

She'd tried to keep the tears back, but the diagnosis and her aunt's impending decline were too close. She wrapped her arms around her waist and squeezed her eyes tightly closed.

Aunt Matilda's diagnosis had given Haley focus. Her aunt had been there when Haley had moved to Redbud Trails during senior year. She'd offered her niece a home when Haley's footloose father had been ready to move on. They'd talked on the phone every week since Haley had gone off to college. And she'd offered Haley emotional support when Haley's serious boyfriend Paul had broken things off.

Until now, the breakup and the distance in her relationship with her father had been the biggest problems in Haley's life. But they were minor compared to what Matilda was facing now. Haley was done wallowing in self-pity. When she got back to her life in Oklahoma City, she was moving on.

She held her breath until the impulse to cry passed.

"I'm real sorry to hear that," he said, and his voice was a little gruff. "Your aunt's a classy lady."

She half-laughed, half-hiccuped. "Yes, she is. Anyway"— she waved off the grief—"that's not what I want to talk to you about. Have you seen this?" She tapped the three-ring binder that Livy had been carrying in her backpack.

He came closer, caddy-corner to her at the edge of the table, and looked down at the computer-printed pages. He flipped one, then another, reading over the information slowly.

"What is this?" he asked.

"It's a business plan. It's Livy's."

He looked up sharply. Haley flushed a little, but wouldn't take the nickname back. Katie's daughter had wanted to be called Livy after they'd bonded over their love of cooking.

He looked toward the kitchen, where they could hear Livy humming a little tune.

"For what?" he asked, still looking toward his niece.

"Ice cream."

"She makes a lot of ice cream at home, different flavors, but... She wants to start a business?"

He looked at her with those unfathomable eyes. For a brief moment, an awareness swelled between them. A memory, a connection. Then he blinked, and it dissolved, leaving nothing in its place.

Haley shook away a tic of sadness. "She was trying to get to the bank to ask for a loan. She made up this business plan—it's actually very detailed. I'm surprised at how much work she's put into it. It's impressive for someone her age."

He furrowed his brow. "Shouldn't she want to be a cheerleader or play basketball? You know, do normal kid things?"

Haley winced but tried to cover it with a smile. "She is a normal little girl," she said softly, glancing over her shoulder to make sure Livy wasn't listening. How many times in her own childhood had Haley wanted to fit in with the other kids? And she hardly ever had.

"Some kids want those things," Haley said. "I think some kids know what they want to do with their lives. What did you want to do when you were Livy's age?"

"Play football." By the clenched jaw, she figured he regretted that statement. "I just don't get why she wants to make ice cream. There's already a chain in town."

"Not just ice cream. *Gourmet* ice cream."

He shook his head. "I don't get it."

"It's a different market than fast food," she explained gently.

He exhaled a long, slow sigh, shifting his feet. "How much?"

"Fifteen hundred dollars."

He ran his fingers through his hair. "You've got to be—"

"She's got a restaurant willing to sell her a used blast freezer at a great deal."

"A what?"

"It's a commercial-grade ice-cream maker."

He shook his head, looking down at the papers in the binder.

"I know it's a lot of money." Haley tapped the folder. "She's done some research. She's got great ideas, I think we could work up a marketing plan—"

"Thanks for encouraging her, but I can't afford something like this." He sounded sincere in his thanks, but also discouraged. He ran one hand against the back of his neck, fluffing the bottom of his slightly-too-long brown curls.

"I'd like to do more than encourage her."

He narrowed his eyes. "You want to give my niece fifteen hundred dollars?" he asked slowly. "Why?"

She shrugged. "I'm here for"—she drew a breath—"the summer, probably. I'd kind of like to go into business with her. Be her partner."

"Why?" he repeated.

For Katie, she wanted to say. And for him. For the dreams that had been lost to Katie's pregnancy and untimely death.

But mostly for Livy. When they'd been talking this afternoon, Haley had seen a glimpse of herself in the younger girl—a little girl hungry for love, for someone to believe in her.

"What if she fails? What if you lose all that money?"

"It's just money."

He looked at her like she'd said something crazy.

"Anyway, that's my problem, mine and Livy's."

He was softening. She could see it in the minute drop of his shoulders.

"Whatever happens, it'll be a learning experience for her," she offered.

"Teach her that life's hard," he muttered, looking back down at the table again.

"What if she doesn't fail?"

When he looked up at her, she saw the truth in his gaze. This wasn't the same confident football star she'd known before. Maybe he didn't believe in his own dreams, anymore.

But Livy deserved her chance.

He glanced toward the kitchen again. From where she stood, Haley couldn't see Livy, but knew the girl could probably hear them. He seemed to have the same thought, because he lowered his voice. "If we do this, I'm not letting you take on the whole expense."

Her heart thumped loudly as she heard what he didn't say. "If...?"

He smiled. A sad little half-smile. More a turning up of one side of his mouth. "I shouldn't. This is crazy."

Maybe it *was* a little crazy. It felt more like one of Katie's old schemes than something the responsible, college-educated Haley would do.

But being here for her aunt, coming back to the place where Katie's life had ended too suddenly—both were reminders that sometimes, life didn't give you second chances.

Livy deserved to chase her dreams. Life was too short to waste it.

And Haley was determined Katie's daughter would have the chance. Even if it meant bumping into this handsome cowboy a few more times.

CHAPTER TWO

A week later, Maddox still couldn't quite believe he'd agreed to Haley's wild scheme. Or that Haley had agreed to give his niece that kind of money.

He'd been gone on the harvest crew for four days, arriving home late last night. While he'd been gone, he'd relied on his cousin Ryan to help out and keep Justin in line. At least Olivia hadn't run away again.

After a short night's sleep, Maddox had been out with the cattle since dawn, starting with a headcount and checking fences. Since high school, he'd spent years building the farm back up after his old man had let things get so bad. Maddox had vowed he would never give up on life like his father had.

He'd just ridden his horse into the barn after cooling the animal down when he heard a car pull up in the drive between the house and the barn. Haley had promised to deliver the machine this evening. Olivia had mentioned it about ten times when he'd gone in for lunch earlier.

He stayed with his horse. He wasn't going to rush out to greet her like a high schooler on a first date. Hadn't he behaved like that enough that last summer? He'd stay here in the barn, even if his heart started pounding and his palms slicked with sweat.

Haley was here for Olivia. Maddox was in no shape to be getting interested in a woman. End of story.

Maddox brushed down the horse, keeping his feet planted right where they were. He thought about how she might smile if he went to greet her, how her curls would look in the fading light. He ground his teeth and ran the brush through the horse hair.

"Hey, Mad!" Ryan's voice rang out. His cousin had been over this afternoon, trying for the thousandth time to cheer up Justin. Or get his butt out of that recliner. Or both.

"Your new girlfriend is here!" Ryan called as Maddox tucked his horse back into its stall.

Maddox gave his horse one last pat. "She's not my girl—" He turned and stopped short. "Howdy, Haley."

Ryan jerked a thumb at her. "Followed me out here."

She peeked at him over Ryan's shoulder, grinning.

Something inside him responded, like his insides broke open or something equally corny. Really? He wasn't nineteen anymore.

"You're early," he groused.

She seemed to see right through him, her smile widening. "I couldn't wait any longer. I love ice cream."

"Livy's in the house."

She nodded but didn't seem in any kind of hurry to head that way. She glanced around the interior of the barn, and he followed her gaze, seeing it through her eyes. Ryan boarded a few horses here, and Maddox's four had stuck their heads over the stall doors, craning to see the owner of that female voice. Or maybe it just seemed that way to him.

He was proud of the place. It wasn't new, not by any stretch, but he'd replaced the roof a couple years ago, and it was clean and the animals were well-cared-for.

"You know, I think I only ever came out here once when I knew..." She paused and seemed to shake off the words "Back in high school. The place looks totally different."

"Good." He ran a much tighter ship than his father ever had, and it showed.

"Uh, the junior high principal called again," Ryan said as they headed toward the barn door.

"Something about Livy?" Haley asked.

Maddox shook his head. The man wanted Maddox to teach a class and coach the junior high football team. Mostly coach.

And Maddox might have considered it if he had the college degree everyone in Redbud Trails thought he did. The job wouldn't make him rich, but it would be better than traveling all summer, and it would be a steady supplement to the income they got from the cattle and small crops they were able to raise.

They left the barn behind and crossed the short field toward the house. He noticed the fifteen-year-old Ford she'd parked in the drive, her aunt's truck.

"How big is this ice cream thing?" he asked. He'd cleared a spot on the counter, but maybe he should have asked for dimensions before he agreed to house it in his kitchen.

"Well, it took three college guys to load it in my aunt's truck."

"Sounds like you need me, too." Ryan winked and flexed a bicep.

Maddox rolled his eyes. He might have been worried about Ryan moving in on Haley, except he knew his cousin was hung up on his high school crush. She'd joined the military and had been stationed overseas when she was injured. Now she was in a military hospital stateside. Ryan had been in love with her since high school. Never really looked at another woman.

Haley rounded the truck on the opposite side and threw back a brown tarp, revealing a plastic-wrapped stainless steel box about the size of an ice chest.

"That's it?" he asked. "The magic machine?" *Which cost so much money...*

"Yep. You guys got it?" She didn't wait for an answer. She opened the cab door and stuck her head inside the truck.

The machine was heavier than he thought it would be, and Ryan hopped in the truck bed to push it toward the edge.

When they hefted it between them, she met them carrying a cardboard box.

"What's that?" he asked.

"Early birthday gift for Olivia."

He opened his mouth to protest, but Ryan shifted the machine, jiggling it. "Mad, c'mon. This is heavy. Let's move."

He ground his back teeth and headed for the house.

She trailed them toward the porch steps, a couple steps behind.

"Do you really call him that?" she asked.

"Everyone else calls him Mad Dog. High school football nickname," Ryan grunted. "Why?"

"It seems like it would be a self-fulfilling prophecy. Like if you expect him to be *Mad*, he will be. Why not something like Joy or Sunshine?"

She said it with such a straight face that at first Maddox didn't catch that she was joking.

Ryan burst out laughing.

She quirked a smile at Maddox, and he almost missed the first step. He bobbled but caught himself with only a knock of one knee on the porch post.

"I suppose it is kind of a natural evolution from *Maddox*. But still...what's your middle name?"

Maddox wasn't saying.

"William," Ryan offered.

They finally cleared the stairs, and Maddox realized she would have to open the door for them. He moved forward, shoving the machine into his cousin's chest in retaliation for making fun of him.

Ryan's eyes danced.

"Hmm...you could've been a Will. Not a Billy," she said as they carried the machine past her and through the living room and on into the kitchen.

"Why not shorten it to *Ox*?" he muttered. "That's what I feel like right now.".

Ryan froze, bringing the two of them up short, and looked at him over the top of the machine with an odd look on his face. Olivia, who was sitting on the far side of the counter, dropped her jaw.

Then his cousin laughed, a surprised burst of sound. "Did you just crack a joke?" Ryan asked.

Maddox ignored him as they maneuvered around the island to the space he'd cleared on the back counter. Finally, he put the machine down, arms aching, and turned to see Haley smiling down at the countertop.

"Who told a joke?" Justin asked, limping into the room, one crutch under his arm. He'd actually come out of his seclusion to watch the spectacle?

"Uncle M, I think," Olivia piped, her face scrunched in confusion.

The tips of Maddox's ears got hot. Had it really been such a long time since he'd made a wisecrack?

Luckily, Olivia's excitement seemed to distract his brother and cousin. She rushed to the machine, bumping past Maddox's elbow in the process. He overheard Haley murmur a soft 'hello' to his brother as she set her box down on the island counter.

Olivia started tugging at the plastic, but it wasn't coming off easy.

"Do you have some scissors? A box knife?" Haley asked.

"I'll do it," Ryan said cheerfully, digging in his jeans' pocket and coming up with a pocketknife. "Then I've got to get to the Reynolds'."

In moments, the plastic was shredded around the stainless steel box.

"It's awesome," Olivia breathed.

"It's a hunk of metal," Maddox argued. It pretty much was, with a small door on top and some buttons and a dispenser on the front.

Haley wrinkled her nose at him. "Just wait 'til you taste the magic that comes out of this baby." She started removing the plastic wrapping and crumpling the pieces between her hands.

"I'm out," said Ryan with a wave. He slipped through the back door, the girls chorusing "Bye," behind him.

Maddox leaned against the far counter and watched as Haley and Olivia made over the machine, Haley focusing as much on the girl as on the machine in front of them. Maddox wondered if she even remembered he and Justin were in the room. "We'll need to clean it first," she said.

Maddox was surprised his brother was still here. Justin had been a bull rider until that accident. It was one thing to get thrown from a bull, but to be trampled by one, too? It had resulted in a career-ending injury—a fractured pelvis. Now, Justin was all but a hermit, limping around the house and battling depression.

But here he was, easing himself down into a kitchen chair and watching the two girls as they disassembled the guts of the machine and dunked them in a sinkful of hot, sudsy water.

"What flavor are you going to try first?" Haley asked.

"I was thinking about something fun, like this recipe I created for banana split." Olivia's voice sounded metallic as she leaned in close, her arm inside the machine as she extracted its guts.

"But then I thought for the first try, maybe I should go with something standard, like vanilla."

"Can't go wrong with a longstanding favorite," Haley said. She scrubbed one of the parts, then rinsed it and set it on a dishtowel to one side of the sink. She'd made herself right at home. She and Olivia were two of a kind, Olivia's dark curls at Haley's auburn shoulder, both of them washing up.

He'd thought she would drop off the machine and be in a hurry to leave. Apparently he'd been wrong.

And then she looked over her shoulder, right at him. "So what's for supper, boys?"

He hadn't thought she would stay. But Olivia's face was all lit up, and he found himself saying, "I can fire up the grill..."

"Uncle Justin makes a mean barbecued chicken," Olivia said, then sent an uncertain look over her shoulder, as if she might've blundered by saying so.

Justin had been so closed in his own little world since his injury, temper close to the surface and frequently boiling over.

Maddox had shouted louder than a coach from the sidelines after he'd let Olivia ride off to town the other day. The younger man hadn't even noticed she'd been gone, too dazed and drugged on pain meds.

But now Justin met Olivia's gaze squarely, his expression clear-eyed for the first time in a long time.

"If I can get a pretty girl to hold the platter for me, I'll give it a shot."

Haley laughed, drying her hands. She threw her arm around Livy's shoulders. "Do you think he was talking about you or me?"

She wasn't quite the shy girl he remembered. She'd matured, but her gentle spirit was still there. He watched as the girls shifted from the now drying equipment to Olivia's notebook and bent over it.

He could almost feel himself falling for her again.

But that was dangerous.

He wasn't the same boy he'd been back then, either. He was a college dropout whose dreams had been put on hold forever.

He didn't know how to dream anymore.

Even though Justin flirted with Haley under the guise of teasing Livy, she knew he was harmless. There was something broken behind his eyes.

It was Maddox's sometimes-hot, sometimes-angsty gaze that she couldn't ignore.

It sent prickles up the back of her neck and made her fidgety as she and Olivia reassembled the blast freezer. At least she could pretend her fumbling was because the machine was new to them.

Finally, they got it back together.

"This is a great spot for it," she told Olivia. It really was. A wide swath of bare cabinet halfway between the stovetop and sink, with access to the island in the middle of the kitchen.

"Uncle Maddox moved some stuff around so it would fit."

"Oh, he did?"

Now that Olivia had mentioned it, the microwave was a newer model that didn't match the rest of the worn appliances. The microwave had been mounted above the stove, and freshly cut wood showed on the cabinets where he might've cut them to make it fit.

Haley flicked a gaze to Maddox. The tips of his ears had gone pink, just like Olivia's had the other day. An adorable shared family trait.

"Kitchen needed updating," he muttered beneath his breath. "Got to start the grill." He moved away, slipping out the back door.

Justin stayed, pushing himself slowly out of the chair and shuffling around the counter on his crutch. "Outta my way, cuties."

"But we have to start our base," Olivia protested. She was practically vibrating with excitement, bouncing on the balls of her feet.

"If you want my special chicken you've got to let me marinate it for a few minutes, Livy-Skivvy."

"Uncle Justin!" Olivia's token protest and giggle showed she wasn't too old yet for the silly nickname.

"I've got something for you first anyway," Haley said, drawing Olivia away.

A small alcove made a nice breakfast nook, and Haley well remembered sitting at the small, round table with Katie in the wee hours of the night, talking about boys. Dreaming about Maddox.

She shook away the memories and moved her box from the island to the table.

"You brought me something?" The hesitant hope in Olivia's voice pinched Haley's heart.

She sat down and motioned the girl next to her. Olivia stepped up to the table.

"The restaurant was liquidating, so I grabbed them for a great price. You've got to have the right tools, don't you?"

Olivia exclaimed over the stainless steel pans they could use to make an ice bath, the industrial whisk and strainer, and the two pots, all of which Haley had tucked into the cardboard box.

The restaurant owner had given it to Haley for a steep discount, happy to be rid of them.

"Here's the best part," Haley said. She took out the small white gift box she'd tucked in the bottom of the bigger cardboard box.

Olivia unfolded the lid almost reverently. "Is this...what I think it is?"

She took out the child-sized apron that Haley had sewn for her. White with vibrant red flowers all over, ruffled on the edges. Similar to the adult-sized one Olivia had worn at Aunt Matilda's last week, when they'd first bonded over their shared love of food.

And the most important part, in the center of the midsection, an embroidered logo. Olivia's ice cream logo.

The little girl was silent for a long moment, and Haley wondered if something was wrong, until Livy spun and threw her arms around Haley, burying her face against Haley's shoulder.

Haley blinked back the hot moisture that wanted to pool in her eyes. She hadn't meant to get emotional.

"Happy birthday," she whispered.

"Thank you, thank you!" Olivia came away, slipping the apron over her head and reaching behind to tie the bow. She danced over to her uncle at the counter. "Uncle Justin, look!"

He smiled his approval.

Olivia ran outside, calling, "Uncle Maddox..." her voice faded as the screen door slammed behind her.

And Haley was left alone with Maddox's younger brother.

She let her eyes skim around the room. It was much the same as she remembered, the pale green walls, the same cabinets and countertops. The womanly touches were gone. There was still a dishtowel hanging from a towel rack where Katie's mother had always kept it, but all of her knickknacks were gone.

It was plain, but homey, too. Comfortable.

And then she had nothing else to look at but Justin. He continued working with the raw chicken breasts on the cutting board, but he must've sensed her perusal.

"Nice gift," he said. "Nice of you to give her the machine, too."

She couldn't tell from the sound of his voice whether he really thought it was nice, or he was being sarcastic.

She'd asked Aunt Matilda about him after Maddox's

mention of his injury. But she didn't know if she should ask about his recovery or leave it alone.

"I'm excited to work with Livy," she said simply.

"It's not exactly a lemonade stand."

"You sound like Maddox," she said before she'd really thought about the words. The other night, Maddox had been more than concerned about Livy's venture. He'd been negative, though at least he hadn't said anything to the girl.

"I was sorry to hear about your accident."

"Wasn't an accident," he drawled. "Bull knew what it was doing when it stepped on me."

"Oh." What else to say to a remark like that? She listened to the scraping of the knife against the cutting board, the ticking of the clock on the far wall. What was taking Olivia so long?

She brightened her voice. "So what're you doing these days?"

His kept his focus on the chicken, but she saw his face crinkle in a smile. It wasn't a nice smile, more like a fierce baring of his teeth.

"That's the question, isn't it? And the answer is *nothing*. I sit around all day in my pop's old recliner and watch soap operas."

"Um..."

The waves of anger radiating off of him were almost palpable. But there was something deeper underneath. Desperation.

"Livy said you helped her with a school project. So that's something."

"Hmm. Well, maybe I could have a career tutoring kids. Oh, except I barely graduated high school."

She didn't know how to handle his anger and sarcasm. If he was one of her friends back in the city, she would be comfortable enough to offer an alternative. To say *something*.

"They have adult education scholarships," she said softly.

"What?" he barked.

She cleared her throat. "Scholarships," she forced the word out louder. "You could go back to school. The state university isn't too far from here."

"Did you hear me say I barely made it out of high school?"

She shrugged. "Doesn't mean you wouldn't do all right now. Especially as an older student."

"I'm not *that* much older," he muttered to the chicken.

Finally, Maddox and Livy returned, the girl wearing her apron and chattering excitedly.

Maddox looked between Justin and Haley. Thankfully, he didn't say anything.

But she wasn't sure how long that could last.

"So...thanks for bringing the freezer blaster thing out," Maddox said.

Haley laughed. "Blast freezer. You're welcome." She slipped out the Michaels' front door and down the porch steps, Maddox following.

The last bit of white light hung on the horizon as twilight deepened around them.

"The ice cream was...good," he said.

She glanced over at him, incredulous. She'd seen him palm a lightswitch as they exited the house, and now the porch light illuminated his faint smile and the day's growth of beard.

"Okay." His lips twitched. "It was better than good."

"It's incredible," she said. "And so is Livy."

She thought they had a real shot at making Livy's business a success. With Haley's education and her job as a marketing assistant back in Oklahoma City, and Livy's ingenuity, especially when it came to flavors, they had a chance.

He followed her to the truck, their shoes crunching in the gravel. She breathed in the cool country night air, nothing like the urban scents she was accustomed to in Oklahoma City.

"It must be hard to be away from her, traveling so much."

It must be difficult, period, for a man raising a young girl and trying to be an emotional support for his brother.

Maddox said nothing.

He'd been friendly enough over supper, asking about Haley's job and life back in Oklahoma City. But now he was quiet, pensive.

Haley had seen Livy's breathless hope when she'd presented the ice cream to her uncle. She remembered having that same gut-clenching feeling toward her own father. Whether she'd been handing him her report card or a cookie she'd baked herself, she'd wanted her father's approval, needed the emotional connection.

Maddox had praised the ice cream. But Haley also remembered that Livy hadn't gone to her uncle with the business plan.

And Haley wanted Livy to have that special connection with her uncle.

"I would have loved a childhood like this," she said, too vulnerable to look him in the face. She stared instead at the stars above the roof of the barn.

He snorted. "What, growing up with two bachelors?"

"Growing up with roots," she said softly.

He rested one palm on the top of the truck bed, and she leaned against the side and continued staring into the heavens. Another thing she missed living in the city—the bountiful stars.

"My dad and I moved around so much when I was growing up, I never felt like I belonged anywhere. You can give that to Livy. Roots."

"How come your dad didn't settle down?"

She shrugged. "He was always chasing...something. The next promotion. A different job..."

She breathed in deeply. "At first, I let myself get too attached to places. Found best friends. Settled into school. But I was never enough to make him stay. Or, my needs weren't..."

She felt it when he turned his head to look at her. A flare of heat hit her face.

"And I don't know why I'm telling you all this." She dusted off her hand on her jeans nervously and glanced at him. "I'm over it now. I have friends, good friends in Oklahoma City. I'm happy there. I'll be going back once Aunt Matilda..." She still couldn't finish the sentence.

"Good for you," he said. "I'm glad."

But he didn't say the same about himself. Why did he work so hard? Was he really happy on the farm, or did he think he didn't have options?

Instead of voicing those questions, Haley asked, "Why do you call her Olivia? In the hospital, I remember Katie calling her Livy."

He moved one arm, palm sliding along the side of the truck. "We don't talk about Katie much."

Why not? The words were on the tip of her tongue, but something zinged inside her. A warning, maybe?

His feet shifted, like he was uncomfortable. "Whatever your reason for doing this...helping Olivia... Just remember, she's a little girl who will still be here when you go back to the city."

He sounded like he thought Haley's presence was going to hurt the girl, but all she wanted was to help.

"If this is some kind of...I don't know...call back to Katie's memory—"

"It's not."

He shook his head, gripping the top of the truck bed. "I can't help remembering how you two were thick as thieves..."

Tag-along. His words doused ice water on her. She'd had a wonderful evening with Livy, cooking the first ice cream base and teasing Maddox...

And he still thought of her as Katie's tag-along, after all these years.

She didn't know what to say.

He seemed to understand her sudden uncertainty, because he went on. "Look, I'm just trying to protect my niece. I appreciate that you're trying to do something nice for her."

She waited for the *but*. And it came.

"But giving her that money...building up her dreams..."

"I'm not doing it for Katie. I'm doing it for Livy. We're partners."

Nearby, something rustled in the darkness against the side of the house. It moved, but she couldn't make out the form in the darkness. Whatever it was, it was big.

She thought Maddox was arguing with her, but her

thundering heartbeat drowned out anything he might've said. The Thing padded closer, quiet in the darkness. Were those fangs, glimmering in the dim porch light?

She grabbed his arm, ducking between him and the truck, turning her shoulder away from the animal's hot breath against her side. Was it a Rottweiler? Or just a huge mutt?

"Maddox," she hissed. Her breath came in gasps, fear overpowering her sense of propriety and personal space.

He brought his other arm down, caging her in. "What's the matter?"

"P-please tell me that's a friend."

He looked down, over the side of his arm, then tilted his chin back to her, the light from the corner of the house shining behind him and leaving his face in shadow. "You're still afraid of dogs?"

"I'm n-not afraid. Terrified."

He snorted.

"Git on, Emmie," he said softly.

The huge black dog sat, tail swishing audibly over the gravel of the drive. Its lips parted in a panting, doggie grin. The dim porch light showed that it lifted one paw in a polite shake.

"Git on," Maddox said again, his voice laced with humor.

The dog closed its mouth with a *huff* of air, stood, and sauntered off, fading into the darkness.

And then the man turned his gaze back on her. She looked up at Maddox in the moonlight, and her stomach swooped low, the same way it had when he'd held her on prom night all those years ago.

She could see the dark stubble of his days' growth of beard. His eyes were unreadable in the darkness.

If she wanted to, she could reach up and put her arms around his neck, stand on tiptoe...and claim the second kiss she'd been dreaming about for a dozen years.

But she wasn't seventeen anymore.

And he probably didn't think about her that way. They both had Olivia's best interests at heart.

And Haley wanted to protect her own heart, too.

36

His hands came to rest gently on her waist, but before he could push her away, Haley stepped out of the circle of his personal space. Her heart beat and pulsed in her throat, and it sounded a little like the taunt she always heard in her head. *Tagalong.*

"Thanks for supper. I had a fun time."

She thought he said *me too*, but she tucked herself in the cab of her truck and started the engine. She waved, smiling out the window into the dark so he wouldn't know how shaken the moment had left her.

She wasn't a little sheep any longer. She had her own friends back in Oklahoma City. She wasn't *desperate* for company, no matter what he thought.

She would do what she said. She would see him peripherally while helping Olivia with her ice cream business. She would care for her aunt and mind her own business.

And they could both pretend that the near-embrace never happened.

Maddox stood staring after Haley's taillights long after they'd disappeared down the dirt drive, hands fisted loosely at his sides.

What had he been thinking? He'd *touched* her. She'd been so close, and he'd wanted her closer—wanted to find out if her lips still tasted like the ice cream they'd shared.

But the moment he'd given in to the urge and reached for her, she'd backed away.

He knew better than to reach. Hadn't his past taught him anything?

He didn't have time for any kind of relationship and didn't need Haley nosing into his business.

She wanted him to give Olivia roots. How was he supposed to do that, when he could barely keep them afloat? He wasn't doing that good a job keeping Justin from sinking further into depression, and had a hard time keeping ahead of the medical bills.

He didn't know how to be a father to a little girl.

What did he have to give to Olivia? He was on the road or working dawn-to-dusk, just to make ends meet.

The expectations were too heavy. They had been ever since his teen years, when his mom had turned him into the man of the family. As if he could handle it, because no one else was there to do it. He'd just been a kid when his dad had died in a drunken stupor. He'd been a kid when they'd all expected him to become some kind of football star, and a kid when Katie had left him with a tiny bundle of pink. If love had been enough, he'd have been the best uncle in the world.

But what he'd learned was that his love and his desire to do the right thing weren't enough. He had to be better.

He was a mess, his thoughts churning with the burn in his gut, but no antacid would repair this mess. The last thing he needed was Haley around, tempting him to dream. If he had any brains at all, he'd tell Haley not to come to the house again, but...

She was good for Olivia. That was easy to see. She'd had all three of them, him, Olivia, and even Justin for a few minutes, laughing in the kitchen like a real family.

And Olivia had soaked it up like a parched field in a rainstorm.

He was afraid he had, too.

When was the last time they'd felt like a family, not just individuals living in the same house?

He'd promised himself never to end up like his dad, always stuck in the could-have-beens. Maddox was making a life for Olivia, doing what he could.

It would have to be enough.

But what if it wasn't?

CHAPTER THREE

Three weeks later, Maddox turned down the dirt lane toward home, fresh off of another four-day-stint on the harvest crew. He'd gotten up in the middle of the night and driven all morning to make it here by lunchtime.

The more he'd thought about the things Haley had revealed about her own childhood that night after supper, the more he'd been determined to prove that he could be the father-figure Olivia needed. He could do better than he had been doing. And being here today was a part of that.

Olivia and Haley had planned some elaborate birthday celebration. He thought they might've invited the entire elementary school. They were calling it a *business expense*, planning to do something with all the ice cream they'd made over the last few weeks.

Maddox had never seen so much of the sweet treat in his life. Olivia had been furiously mixing up batches, trying out new flavors with her old personal-sized ice cream maker, and hand-packing quart after quart in cardboard containers.

She'd even appropriated a deep freezer from a neighbor who wasn't using it any more. She already had that sucker half-full.

On one of his at-home breaks, he'd sat down with Olivia and talked about the three books her school had assigned as suggested summer reading. He'd asked about her friends, expecting her to duck his question. Instead, she'd chatted with him for almost an hour. Opened up to him, and all it had taken was him asking.

Haley had been at the house two Saturdays in a row, according to Justin. Maddox had been out with the crew both times.

During those long rides on the combine, he'd imagined his brother spending time with Haley. Justin had been known for his charming ways on the rodeo circuit. Unfortunately, thinking about the two together made Maddox need to pop an antacid. And he knew why.

Haley was special. Maddox had known it when she was seventeen, and he knew it now.

Knowing he was going to see her again today had him antsy and uncomfortable. And he had no business thinking about her like he was. He was barely keeping the farm afloat. Barely avoiding the creditors calling about the overdue medical bills.

Where he'd given up on his dreams, Haley had a fancy degree and no doubt fancy friends in the city. She even cooked fancy.

Even if he did find the guts to pursue her, what would she want with a farmer like him?

She was too good for him. The smartest thing to do would be to forget about her.

But Justin had seemed more grounded after her visits. Less stuck inside his own head. Maddox couldn't help wondering what passed between them.

He turned into the drive to see five farm trucks already parked in a snaking line.

"What the—?" He guided his truck around the outside, half-driving in the ditch so he could get to the house.

He would have sworn Olivia had told him the party would begin in the afternoon.

He parked his truck on the side of the barn, since apparently they were going to need most of the yard for guests.

"Mad, you're here!" Ryan's voice rang out, quickly followed by Olivia's, "Uncle Maddox!"

He braced one hand on his truck and caught Olivia with the other arm when she launched at him. She rubbed her face against his chest. "You made it!"

"I promised, didn't I?"

When she moved back, squealing with excitement, her face was shining. He was stiff and exhausted from driving most of the night, but it was worth it.

When she ran off, he looked up to see Haley standing right there, her eyes showing her surprise.

"Didn't think I'd make it, huh?" he asked.

"I'm glad you did." She seemed sincere, and his heart thumped once hard beneath his breastbone.

She led him to a picnic table that hadn't been in the yard before, beneath a tree that would shade him from some of the hot June sun. "Where'd this come from?" he asked.

"Neighbors," she answered. "Borrowed them."

That's when he saw there were ten tables arranged in a horseshoe.

And the yard had been mowed. "Who mowed?"

"Your brother." She nodded toward the row of trucks, where not only was Justin outdoors, he was leaning on his crutch, talking to old man Simpson. The grocer had been a friend of their mom's and Maddox guessed he had delivered one of the picnic tables.

It was the first time Maddox had seen Justin willingly engage with someone outside their family circle since his fall.

Haley was still talking. "He said, and I quote, *'I can drag along behind the push-mower just as well as I can drag behind my crutch.'*"

He could imagine his brother saying that. Somehow, Haley had gotten him to mow the yard. He hated to think how, but the image of the two flirting with each other came unwelcome into his mind.

"I'm so glad you're here," Haley said, interrupting his thoughts. "I need your help. Have a seat."

In the next few minutes, Haley showed him how she wanted him to slice about thirty watermelons. It seemed like they were planning for a horde—he hoped Haley and Olivia weren't disappointed.

Haley tilted her head to the side, looking at him for a long moment. "You good?" Haley asked.

"Fine."

He didn't like the hot knot that had settled behind his sternum, thinking about her and Justin together. As he watched under the guise of cutting into one of the melons, she got some kind of magazine out of her aunt's truck. Haley marched up to his brother and slapped the book into his stomach.

His brother hugged her briefly around the shoulders, like he would've hugged Katie or their mom, and just kept on talking.

"They're just friends," Ryan said, voice low. Maddox hadn't heard him walk up.

He clapped a hand on Maddox's shoulder. "At first, I thought the same thing you were thinking, but she doesn't look at him the way she looks at you."

Maddox's stomach swooped at that thought. He'd been half in love with Haley when he'd known her as Katie's friend— and the woman she was now affected him just as powerfully.

Ryan had been checking on Justin and Olivia on the weekends Maddox had to be gone, so he must have known what he was talking about.

But it didn't make Maddox feel that much better.

Haley dashed by his table a little later and left a sampler plate of the ice cream. This had been their plan all along. Invite people for free ice cream.

He grabbed Olivia when she tried to skip by. After he'd complimented her on the ice cream, which was delicious, he asked. "How much is this costing?"

"Haley says you have to spend money to make money."

He just hoped they weren't spending too much.

He'd barely gotten started slicing the watermelons when cars began arriving. He smiled and greeted Olivia's guests, shocked at how many came. And kept coming. They seemed to arrive by the van-load. A lot of people he knew from church but hardly greeted on Sundays. People he'd gone to high school with that now had children in elementary school.

Olivia and Haley were in their element, whirling through the crowd, dispensing ice cream and chatting with everyone.

He'd never seen either of them like this before. Haley had always been so shy. Apparently, she'd overcome that. And Olivia...watching Olivia was like seeing Katie alive again. It made his heart thump painfully.

Just a month before, his niece had been a sad little girl, defensive and lonely. Then she met Haley, and everything changed. Haley seemed to be exactly what Olivia needed. His little girl was blooming with Haley around. But how long was she going to stay?

Haley couldn't believe it. When Maddox had promised to be there, she'd envisioned comforting a very disappointed Olivia. Instead, Maddox had driven all night to be at Livy's party.

Her own father would never have done something like that.

She couldn't help it that her gaze kept straying to him during the hot afternoon. She saw plenty of folks greet him, many slapping him on the shoulder while he shook their hand.

She also saw the lines of stress around his mouth. But she didn't know why. Was it the money? Trying to run the farm while he supported Justin and Livy?

She'd barely seen him since their dinner together, but Livy had told her all about how they'd spent extra time together recently. The way Olivia talked about him, it was obvious the girl thought he hung the moon. And Justin had a grudging respect for him, even through his pain and depression.

Haley's high school crush had never completely gone away—and now it was back with a vengeance. She'd buried it under her busyness and college life. And that doomed relationship with Paul. Paul, who'd always made her feel like she wasn't good enough for him.

Watching Maddox now, she could see that he was still the same popular jock, but beneath that hard exterior lurked something darker. And she couldn't help wondering what it was.

By midafternoon, Haley needed a break. She'd been on her feet since this morning. She spotted a chance and plopped down on the bench beside Maddox, bumping his shoulder with hers. "Hey."

"Hey," he responded.

The top of the picnic table was covered with sticky juice from the watermelons and Haley was careful to keep clear of it.

Olivia showed no signs of fading. She spun from one person to the next, bubbly and grinning.

The little girl had been keeping count of the number of samples they'd handed out. They'd come up with the idea of purchasing small disposable condiment bowls and scooping samples into them. Each partygoer got a sampler plate, so they could try several different flavors.

And they'd printed quarter-sheet flyers listing the flavors and ordering instructions, which they'd handed out with each sample.

The response had been wonderful. People had marveled at all Livy had done, at the wonderful ice cream, and at the girl's ingenuity. Haley couldn't have been more pleased.

"She seems happy," Maddox said, voice low. "And I can't believe Justin was out here for awhile. What did you give him earlier?"

"Hmm?" She was so tired, she couldn't think straight.

"Earlier, I watched you hand him something. Looked like a magazine or—"

"College catalog. I've almost convinced him to enroll for the fall."

Maddox shifted to look into her face. "You're kidding."

He didn't seem particularly happy about it. The lines around his mouth had tightened even more.

"Hey, Katie's friend!" The voice came from a little cluster of folks near the back porch, and then a woman walked up to their table, waving off one of the last slices of watermelon that Maddox tried to slide across to her.

Haley froze, then forced a smile to her face. She recognized the woman from high school but couldn't remember her name, either. She shouldn't have been surprised to be called, "Katie's friend," even after all these years. Apparently, Haley would always be the *tag-along* in this town.

"Can I buy a quart today?" the woman asked.

"We hadn't planned to sell any until next week."

Maddox snorted. "Olivia's been running that machine night and day. I bet I could find a quart for you to take home. How much are you willing to pay for it?"

"You gonna auction off some ice cream, Mad Dog?" a man Haley didn't know asked, wandering closer from the crowd around the porch.

Maddox looked at Haley, something brewing behind his eyes.

He stood up, using the table for leverage, then bellowed, "Livy!"

The girl darted out of the crowd, beaming and wearing the apron Haley had made her.

She approached, and Maddox whispered something to her. She squealed and ran off to the kitchen.

While she was gone, Maddox started clearing off the picnic table. Haley helped, but when she asked what he was up to, he half-grinned and said nothing.

A few minutes later, Livy climbed on top of the picnic table, and Haley realized what Maddox and Livy had planned. They were auctioning off five quarts of the gourmet ice cream. Immediately, a crowd gathered around.

Olivia's eyes were shining, but Maddox looked slightly pained.

Maddox started, "Okay, we've got—" Olivia murmured something to him—"Chocolate covered strawberries, folks. Who'll give me fifteen bucks for this quart?"

It had been one of the most popular flavors of the day, and Haley wasn't surprised to see several hands go up.

Maddox got the bid up to thirty before his voice boomed, "Sold, to the gal in the yellow shirt." Within a few minutes, the rest of the quarts were auctioned and, with some cheesing up to the audience and Olivia chipping in about the ingredients she'd put into each different ice cream, sold for top dollar.

Handing out the prized ice cream, Olivia was bouncing

45

with joy.

Haley watched from the edge of the yard, swelling with pride for Livy. All the work they'd put into this event had been worth it. And when Maddox's eyes met hers, that pride was replaced with something entirely different.

The party was winding down when Haley brought Maddox a bottle of water. He'd been sitting at the same table, though finally, he'd been left alone for a little while. He grabbed the water, twisted off the cap, and downed it. "Thanks."

"You looked thirsty."

He was wiping his mouth with his sleeve when Rob Shepherd, one of the loan officers from the bank, moseyed by.

"Got a neat little operation here," the man said. "I hope it pays off for you."

"It's all Livy," Haley said, sliding onto the bench beside him. Thank God she hadn't caught the man's undertones.

"Place is looking good, Michaels," he said. "I heard the medical bills might keep you from putting in that irrigation system you were talking about last winter."

Maddox could only imagine who he'd heard that from. Small-town gossip.

"Not this year," Maddox said, gritting a smile out.

The other man lifted one foot onto the bench opposite theirs and shot the breeze for another few minutes before moseying off.

"What was that about?" Haley asked.

He shrugged. "Folks around here have a long memory."

She nodded. He guessed she probably understood that, the way everyone still remembered her as Katie's friend.

She narrowed her eyes. "So...?"

"So some of them have been waiting for me to fail, just like my old man."

"Really?" She sounded surprised. "Back then, it seemed like they were all pulling for you."

"Not all of them."

She tilted her head to the side. "Are you sure you're not

projecting?"

"What's that mean?" He shook his head. "Forget it." It was about time to find a trash bag. When he stood, she followed him.

"It means, are you sure *you* aren't the one worried about failing?"

She always did have a way of cutting to the heart of the matter.

He gritted his back teeth. He didn't want to talk about his pop with her. Didn't really want to think about the man—it was a waste of time.

She stopped him in the shade of the house with a soft hand on his sleeve. "No matter what anyone else says or thinks, you've got Livy—you've done a good thing."

The way she was looking at him, like she believed in him.... Suddenly, possibilities rose like a shimmering mirage.

He just didn't know if he had the strength to hope in possibilities any more.

CHAPTER FOUR

Several days after Olivia's birthday, Haley awoke feeling somehow...off, but she couldn't pinpoint why.

It wasn't until she was driving home after picking up some prescriptions for Aunt Matilda that she realized what day it was. The anniversary of the car accident that had killed Katie.

She was coasting past the small town cemetery when she saw a lone, small figure, huddled into herself. Livy.

Grief and hot disappointment surged through her.

Haley parked around the side, not wanting to interrupt the girl.

How could she have almost forgotten such an important day? And where were Livy's uncles?

She had her phone in her hand and dialed before she could talk herself out of it. It really wasn't her business. But she cared about Livy, too.

Maddox picked up on the first ring. "Haley?"

She should've held her tongue, but the words burst out before she could even think.

"How could you leave her alone today? Even if you couldn't bring her—"

"Olivia—?"

"Did she ride her bike to town again? I would've picked her up—"

"Haley—"

"She's at the cemetery, Maddox. By herself. Where are you?"

Her voice broke as she remembered standing alone at her

mother's grave in a St. Louis cemetery, saying goodbye the day before Haley's father moved them across the country.

There was a long pause, as if he were waiting to see if she was really done railing at him.

Then, a quiet. "I'm here."

She scanned the area and saw his truck parked on the opposite side of the fence.

He lifted his hand from the steering wheel in a brief wave.

"She said she wanted to go alone."

The enormity of what she'd done crashed down on Haley. Not only had she ranted at him when he was most likely grieving too, but she'd accused him of neglecting Olivia again, this time when he didn't deserve it.

She squeezed her eyes closed, the hand that wasn't holding her phone squeezing on the steering wheel.

"I'm sorry," she whispered.

When Haley pulled around and parked beside his truck, Maddox wasn't surprised.

She was something of a pit bull beneath that friendly, smiling exterior.

He was starting to like it.

It made his voice gruff when she popped his door open.

She just looked at him for a long moment, silent and assessing.

"You okay?" Her soft-spoken question hit harder than he wanted to let on.

He looked out over the wrist he'd rested on the dash, squinting a little.

Then she shocked him by taking his other hand. Picked it right up off of his thigh, mashing it between both of her smaller, cool hands. Touching him again. Comforting him.

"I'm fine," he said.

But he wasn't. Not really. He'd spent all morning tiptoeing around Justin, who'd been more of a grump than usual.

His brother hadn't talked about the giant elephant in the room, their shared loss. So Maddox hadn't either.

Maddox's chest expanded, and he breathed out harshly.

But he didn't have time for more than that, because she was pulling him out of the truck. "What—?"

"Even if Livy told you she wanted to be alone, that's not what she needs."

He dug in his heels, unease bucking like an unbroken bronco.

She shook her head. "We've got to get you educated on woman-speak before Livy turns into a teenager."

She tugged him forward, and this time he went, mostly to save his wrist from being pulled out of socket.

He didn't know how to handle Olivia's grief. He didn't even know what to do with the hot ball lodged in own his gut.

He wasn't equipped to deal with this. Maybe he never would be.

But somehow... Having Haley at his side made the trek past all those other graves less daunting.

Olivia looked up at their approach, and the pain in her eyes nearly sent him to his knees. But she was dry-eyed, thank God.

Haley let go of his hand, and he felt the loss intensely, but she wrapped both arms around Olivia's shoulders.

The sight of them together, like mother and daughter, made his heart thump once, hard.

"I'm so sorry, baby," she said to Olivia. He could hear the pain in her words.

Olivia must've, too, because she burrowed her head into Haley's shoulder.

Then Haley looked up at him, eyes baring her heart. She motioned him closer, but he hesitated. Could he weather Olivia's emotional storm?

Haley didn't give him a choice. She reached out and grabbed his shirtsleeve and gave him such a hard tug that he stumbled toward both girls. Being close, his only alternative was to put his arms around them.

Olivia turned her face toward him and pressed her cheek into his chest. He tightened his arm around her shoulders. Haley shifted, like she might be trying to back out of the embrace, but he tightened his arm around her, too.

She'd gotten him into this. She was staying.

It felt right, having her in this circle with him.

She looked up at him from entirely too close, and her cheeks were wet. "I miss her, too," Haley whispered.

And darn if he didn't find himself saying, voice rough, "Me, too."

And Olivia burst into tears. She clutched the back of his shirt in one hand.

He looked frantically at Haley, who gave a wet chuckle. She rested her hand on the crown of Olivia's head.

They stayed like that for several minutes, in a tight huddle. Until Olivia's sobs quieted to hiccups and he was sweating through his T-shirt from being so close to two other bodies in the hundred-plus degree Oklahoma sun.

Finally, Olivia pushed away, and he let them both go.

Olivia wiped her face with her fingers, and then Haley pressed a Kleenex she'd pulled from somewhere into his niece's hand.

"Thanks," Olivia said quietly. She didn't look up.

Haley looked at the top of Olivia's head. "I haven't been back here since the funeral."

Olivia's head came up. "You knew my mom?"

Haley glanced at Maddox, then back to the girl. "Yeah. I did. I moved to Redbud Trails halfway through my senior year of high school. We were friends until she died."

Olivia's face lit up. Haley gestured to the dry, sun-baked grass. "You wanna sit for a little bit?"

Maddox made a noise, mostly to discourage her because of her dressy suit pants, but she dragged Olivia down with her and didn't seem worried about her slacks getting grass stains.

He sat with them, folding his too-long legs beneath him to complete their triangle.

"You're a lot like her," Haley said.

"Really?" Olivia's voice cracked, a sound between hope and uncertainty.

His heart ached with some of that uncertainty. Katie had

been an inferno, bright and sometimes painful, burning out too quickly. *How much* was Olivia like her mother?

"Your eyes, your hair, your nose," Haley said. "The first day I saw you, I thought you looked just like her."

He nodded, listening. But not as raptly as Olivia was, with her face turned toward Haley, her eyes glued to her.

"Everyone liked Katie," Haley went on. "Wherever she went, people greeted her by name."

That was true, too.

"On my first day of school, I didn't know a soul. Before my first class was over, Katie had grabbed me and toted me with her down the hall and to our next class. She was so nice... and she didn't take *no* for an answer."

Maddox smiled. "She never did."

Olivia's head swiveled to him, her eyes serious, hopeful...

And he couldn't deny her.

Especially when Haley kicked the toe of his boot.

"She was a prankster. She would put bugs and lizards—one time even a snake—in our boots in the mudroom. Justin and I learned to check them every time."

Olivia giggled. He and his brother had never learned to laugh at her jokes. They'd always complained loudly to their mom.

He leaned back, letting his wrist take his weight. Some of the painful pressure in his chest was deflating, like a slow helium leak from a balloon.

"She was great at math and science, like you, Olivia," Haley remembered. She leaned back on her arm as well, her fingers overlapping Maddox's on the ground. Had she done that on purpose?

"And she was a planner, too," Haley continued. "She worked for weeks on what we were going to wear to prom, where we would eat supper, who we were going with..." She trailed off, a beautiful pink flush spreading across her face.

She must've realized exactly who she was talking to.

Maddox found himself grinning. She was finally getting a taste of her own medicine—the discomfort he'd felt ever since she'd burst into his life in vibrant color.

"She was a good friend." Haley sniffed, and he realized she was blinking back tears.

Olivia sniffled as well.

"And she loved, you, kiddo," he said, through a sandpaper throat. "In the hospital with you, those first few days... she barely let anyone else hold you. She didn't want to let you go, even for a minute."

Olivia was crying again, silent tears streaming down her face, looking at him like...like she almost didn't believe him. "Why did she have to die?" she whispered.

He gathered her up, more natural about it this time. He shook his head, held her tightly. "I don't know, kiddo, I don't know."

Haley was wiping her eyes as unobtrusively as she could, but she was staying, sticking by his side, even though she probably needed to get back to her aunt.

But she was still here. When it hurt.

She placed a hand on Olivia's back, offering comfort.

Because Olivia needed her.

And then she reached out and touched his upper arm. Offering the same.

Because...he needed her.

Their eyes met and held. His insides churned like he'd ridden a whirly carnival ride. She did that to him. Discombobulated him until he wasn't sure which way was up.

But she also comforted him in a way no one else could.

She touched him, when no one else did.

He couldn't be...falling for her. Again. Could he?

He bent his head down over Olivia, the brim of his hat breaking the fragile connection of their gaze.

His heart was thundering now, he was sweating more than the baking sun really called for.

He wasn't falling for her. He couldn't be. She was just Katie's old friend. Now Olivia's friend. She'd helped him comfort Olivia, and he was grateful. That was all.

Right?

CHAPTER FIVE

"Are you going out to the Michaels' place today?"

Several days after the emotional scene at the cemetery, Haley settled in the floral-covered chair next to her aunt's bedside. The lunch she'd brought on a tray earlier lay on the bedside table, mostly untouched. She would take it back to the kitchen in a minute, but as long as Aunt Matilda was awake, she would sit and talk for a bit.

"I don't know."

Haley couldn't get Maddox off her mind. He and Livy were making strides from where they'd been at the beginning of the summer, when she'd come back into their lives.

He'd been calling the little girl every night from the road on the harvest crew.

And the last two nights, he'd called Haley. They'd talked for close to an hour each time, about her job as a marketing assistant for a big firm in Oklahoma City. About Justin and the accident and his recovery. About Livy.

But Maddox held back about himself.

"Am I getting too involved?" she asked her aunt. It was somewhat of a rhetorical question. "I started the summer wanting to help Livy with her ice cream business and maybe show her uncle what he was missing out on..."

"And now you've met the real man."

And she was afraid she was falling in love with him.

"I'm glad," Aunt Matilda smiled and a patted Haley's hand. "I was afraid you were going to be hung up on that awful Patrick forever."

"Paul," Haley corrected gently. "And I've been over Paul for a while."

After spending time with Maddox this summer, she wondered if what she'd felt for the other man had been real love. In the beginning, she'd been infatuated with him. But as their relationship wore on, sometimes the things he said made her feel uncomfortable. He didn't think she was outgoing enough. Always wanted to go to more parties, when Haley would be perfectly content to stay home for a quiet dinner. They'd been together for two years and she'd been expecting a proposal. Instead, he'd left her behind for an out-of-state job. She'd *thought* she'd been heartbroken.

But if she'd loved him, why didn't she go with him? He hadn't asked, but what had stopped her from suggesting it?

She didn't know the answer to that question.

And she didn't know what to do about Maddox.

"Open your heart," Aunt Matilda said. "Don't be afraid to fall in love again. Life's too short to miss your second chances."

Coming from her aunt, the words were a bittersweet reminder.

The doorbell rang.

"Expecting someone?" her aunt asked.

"No."

When she pulled open the front door, there were Maddox and an effervescent Livy on the front stoop.

"What are you doing here?"

Livy's answer was a hug that Haley gratefully accepted. A step behind, Maddox held up a hand-packed quart of ice cream in each hand.

"New flavor, and we thought we'd better check on you and Mrs. Matilda."

It was thoughtful...and unexpected.

"Can I take it in to Aunt Matilda?" Livy asked, bouncing on her toes. Bubbling with energy, as usual.

Haley agreed. "Grab a spoon from the kitchen," she called after the girl.

Maddox relinquished the carton to her and trailed her into the kitchen. They passed Livy on her way to Matilda's room.

Haley fished a pair of spoons out of the silverware drawer and offered one to Maddox.

"I shouldn't," he said, but he took the spoon anyway. "I had a taste at home already." He patted his stomach, and she rolled her eyes.

"It would take more than a taste to fatten you up. You work too hard."

A shadow flickered in his eyes, but he only smiled.

"So what flavor do we have here?" Haley dipped her spoon in what looked like a swirl of vanilla and caramel, but was... "Pumpkin bread?" she asked in surprise after the first bite.

"Yes, and it's addictive."

She sighed as she swallowed a few good bites. "This was just what I needed today." Both the ice cream and the visit.

"Glad we could oblige." His voice was a rumble of laughter, and Livy's giggle from the bedroom was an echo of the same.

He set the spoon down in the stainless steel sink. "Do you want to come to a rodeo this weekend? Like a... date?"

The tips of his ears had turned that endearing red.

"I thought you were on the road again."

"The kid I'm splitting shifts with needed to switch our days. I'll get back out there next week. Plus, I wanted to spend a little more time with Livy. School will start soon."

Their eyes met, and she read his sincerity. He was really trying with Livy.

He'd even changed his schedule.

Maybe he was figuring out that you never got back that lost time.

And she realized she didn't want to lose any time, either. No matter the risk.

She agreed in a whisper. "All right."

CHAPTER SIX

Two days later, the realization that Matilda didn't have much time left finally became real for Haley.

She curled in a ball on the living room sofa and cuddled beneath one of Aunt Matilda's afghans, idly flipping through a photo album. She had rarely seen her aunt during her childhood, with her father moving the two of them around often. Until her senior year of high school, when Aunt Matilda had asked her to stay. They'd become close, almost as close as the mother she'd missed for years. Even when Haley had gone to college and made her life in Oklahoma City, they'd kept in touch with frequent phone calls and Matilda's visits to the city.

Unlike Haley's father, who had grown more and more distant. She might talk to him once every three months. At Christmas. Aunt Matilda had become the parent Haley needed.

What was Haley going to do without her? She still thought of Aunt Matilda's house as *home*, even after a decade away.

It was after nine when the soft knock came. At first she thought she'd imagined it.

But when it came a second time, she knew that whoever was out there wasn't going away. She peeked out the peephole to see Maddox's strong features and opened the door without thinking. It was when he blinked, visibly surprised, that she remembered she was wearing her painting sweatpants and rattiest T-shirt, she hadn't had a shower, her hair was tucked in a messy ponytail, and she probably had bags under her eyes.

It had been that kind of day.

His eyes softened when he saw her.

She tried to smile, but the weight of the day filled her eyes with tears.

She raised a hand to cover her face or ward him off—she hadn't completely made up her mind which—but he took her elbow in one of his big hands and tugged her forward.

He wrapped her in his muscled arms, and she sank into his embrace. She let him take her weight, buried her face in his chest, and breathed in leather and horse and cowboy.

"Bad day, huh?"

His words were a rumble under her cheek and hot in her hair and she hung on tightly.

She nodded, the top of her head bumping his chin.

"She's hanging in there?"

She nodded again. "Getting weaker," she said against the collar of his T-shirt.

"Still doesn't want to go to the hospital?"

This time she shook her head. Tears burned her eyes. The end was nearing for her aunt, but Haley wasn't ready to let her go.

He held her, giving her his strength. She knew she couldn't have him, not really. He was firmly anchored here in Redbud Trails, and she was eventually going back to her life in Oklahoma City. But she could have tonight.

When she'd settled a little, his hands moved to her waist, clasping her loosely.

She let go of him and raised both hands to wipe her cheeks.

Then he tipped her chin up, used the pad of his thumb to catch the tears she'd missed.

As she looked at those infinite brown eyes, shadowed in the darkness, he slid his palm against her jaw and leaned in.

And kissed her.

Minutes later—Maddox couldn't tell you how many—they sat together on the porch swing. He'd given Haley the quart of ice cream Olivia had sent, and she'd brought out two spoons, but he'd barely tasted the half-melted sweet. He wanted to remember the taste of Haley, not ice cream.

"How'd you know I needed this tonight?" she asked. Her head lolled on his shoulder, and his arm rested around her.

They fit perfectly together.

Just like at her senior prom.

Except for the fact that she was leaving, and he was stuck here in Redbud Trails, trying to save the family farm, trying to keep his brother afloat, trying to be a father to Olivia.

"Olivia saw me heading out the door and wanted you to try it. Sorry if it's melted."

"I'm not." The smile in her voice made him smile, too, and he squeezed her shoulders.

"What's she calling it?"

He wanted to ask her about her aunt again, but he knew how sometimes when you were so deep in something, you just needed to think and talk about the silly little things in life.

So that's what he gave her.

"She said 'peach cobbler'."

"Mmm. I like it. I predict it will be popular."

He shook his head. "You'd predict that about any of her creations."

"I would not. Not the bad ones."

Haley's early predictions about the business had been right. Things were taking off. Orders kept coming in, and Olivia spent hours running her machine. She was talking about maybe needing a second deep freezer. And she was thrilled about it.

Finally finished, Haley set the quart on the floor near their feet, and when she straightened, she turned so they were almost face-to-face and laid her palms on his cheeks.

He jumped from the cold.

She giggled. "Sorry."

But she wasn't really. He took her cold hands in his and rubbed them, providing friction, and he hoped, warmth. He was certainly warm enough for the both of them.

"Can I ask you something?"

"Yeah."

"How come you've never talked about Katie? With Livy, I mean."

He breathed in deep. "After she died, Livy was so little. Mom couldn't bear to talk about her. Those first months were hard on all of us. Then mom had her stroke and just gave up, and Justin and I didn't talk about anything. We were focused on surviving.

"I guess I never realized Livy needed it. Not until you came along. Now she wants to hear about Katie all the time."

She smiled against his shoulder.

"Has Justin picked out any classes for the fall?"

"Yeah. But he still has to go to the school and register."

Maddox wasn't ready to believe that his brother would do it. But Justin was at least talking about getting back to having a life instead of moping around in that recliner all day.

It was an improvement, if a small one. Haley had made her mark there, too.

The tip of his boot dragged on the porch floor. Their swing barely moved. She didn't seem to mind.

"Don't forget about our date Saturday. Do you still think you'll be able to come?"

"Unless Aunt Matilda gets much worse. She's looking forward to hearing all about it."

"Good."

He tucked her close again and rested his chin on top of her head. He liked being with her like this. He could imagine spending all their summer nights together, talking about their days and just *being together*.

He wanted it. Wanted it so bad he could taste it.

And that was just plain dangerous.

But it didn't stop him.

Haley was wide-awake when Maddox left a half hour later. She needed sleep, but instead of climbing into bed, she stared out the window where his taillights had disappeared.

She was in love with him.

Forget about a teenager's crush on her friend's handsome older brother.

She'd seen the real man. Someone who worked his butt off

to take care of his family. Someone who held her, not asking for anything. Giving comfort.

Someone real.

Not the dream she'd imagined for so long.

How was she going to go back to her old life after this was all over?

CHAPTER SEVEN

Saturday came, right on the heels of a new pile of medical bills. Maddox had thought they'd gotten through all of them, but a phone call to their insurance company revealed the truth—here was another stack waiting to be paid.

He'd gotten complacent these last few days, talking with Haley on the phone. Kissing her.

Thinking that they might have some kind of future together.

What had he been thinking?

He had a kid, a brother, and a farm to take care of, and bills out the wazoo.

Later that night, when Haley joined him and Justin and Livy at the rodeo arena one town over, those thoughts kept him company. He couldn't get past them even though to make polite conversation.

She noticed. Of course.

Sitting next to him on the crowded bleachers, she bumped his knee with hers, smiling sideways at him. Livy was on her other side, and Justin took up another seat past her. Maddox had been shocked when his brother had asked to ride along. He hadn't wanted to get off the farm at all, and now he wanted to attend a rodeo?

But Maddox had helped him load his crutches into the truck without a word.

"Did you ever want to do rodeo as a child?" Haley asked.

"For a few weeks," he admitted. He squinted down at the action in the fenced-off, dirt-packed arena. A bell rang and a horse took off from the starting gate at one side, its rider clinging to the reins and urging it on as it raced around three barrels in a triangle, then back out the gate where it had started.

"What happened?" Haley asked after the barrel rider had finished her loop.

"Took a ride on a sheep. Fell off, and decided football was safer."

"That's my brilliant brother," Justin put in from Livy's other side.

Maddox let Justin take the conversational reins, talking about their childhood and Katie riding barrels.

Until Haley bumped him again. "Wanna take a walk? I'll buy you a pretzel."

He considered her. She was wearing a cute pair of jeans, boots, and a black Stetson he'd never seen before. It made her look right at home in this crowd. "This is my date. I'm buying."

She met his gaze squarely. "I'm glad you remembered," she teased softly.

She was right. He'd let his worry about the medical bills take over his thoughts.

But it was also his life. He had to support his family. He refused to do what his dad had done and give up.

She followed him down the bleachers, and when he started off to the food trucks, she slid easily under his arm. Her boots put the top of her head level with his chin, and she felt *right* there. Again.

One of Justin's friends called out to Maddox, and he waved, a flop of his hand on her shoulder.

"Wanna tell me what's wrong?" They stood in line behind a few people with the same idea about the pretzels, and she looked up at him with slightly raised brows, waiting for an answer.

"Nothing for you to worry about," he said. "You've got enough going on with your aunt." And being broke wasn't exactly something he wanted to own up to. He had a little pride.

"That's true." Her chin lifted toward him. "But I can still

listen."

He shook his head slightly. Not tonight. His problems were still too raw.

She looked off into the distance. "Once I get back to Oklahoma City, maybe you could drive down for a visit..."

Haley continued to speak, but he heard very little. He'd known she would be leaving, knew this was only temporary, but how could she speak of it so casually? Her words, the very thought of her leaving, felt like a punch in the gut.

It had taken Haley so long to build up the courage to ask him to visit her in the city, and then...nothing. No answer. No response whatsoever.

She'd thought...

She'd hoped his kisses meant something. That his arm around her shoulder, the way he'd comforted her the other night, meant his feelings were growing. Growing to match what hers already were.

And here they were, on a date. A date he'd requested. Not a *let's go as friends* thing, but a real, honest-to-goodness date. And yet...

Had she been kidding herself?

Was he just enjoying a summer romance? Was he being a courteous cowboy, or simply returning her kindness to Livy?

They inched forward in the pretzel line. She took a deep breath, steeling her courage, and looked up at him. He met her gaze, his eyes dark beneath the brim of his hat. He didn't smile, but the corners of his eyes crinkled.

And she knew.

He cared about her.

But something held him back.

The gal behind the counter cleared her throat, and Maddox placed their order. He bought her a paper-wrapped pretzel and a bottle of water and led her away from the crowded line.

"So that's a *no*?" she asked tentatively.

He shook his head slightly. What did that mean? Was it *no*, that his non-response hadn't meant *no*, or just *no* to her question in general?

He led them clear of the crowd, stopped, and faced her. "I'm going to have to pick up some extra work," he said. "I doubt I'll have time to come down, even if it's for a weekend."

Oh. After what he'd said the other night, she'd thought he might be cutting back on extra work.

"Livy needs you," she said in a small voice.

"She also needs new school clothes and a roof over her head," he muttered.

They meandered toward the stands, not in any hurry, finally stopping behind them, in the small patch of shadow. On the other side of the bleachers, the arena lights lit everything, but here it was dark.

"Justin said you might have a lead on a job with Livy's school. Coaching football and teaching a little."

"So y'all have been talking about me?"

"He mentioned it."

Maddox blew out a breath. She couldn't tell if he was frustrated that she'd been in his business or frustrated about the job. "I can't take that job," he said, the anger evident, though she didn't understand it.

"Why not?" She was angry, too, though not for herself. She was trying not to feel anything for herself—the last few minutes had shattered her hopes for anything with him. But Livy needed him. "You'd have more time for Livy, all summer off—"

"I'd still have a farm to manage, but that's not the point. I can't take that job."

"If it's about being on the sidelines—"

"It's not," he said, and his voice rang with hurt.

"About expectations?"

He laughed, a harsh sound.

"You want the truth?" he asked roughly.

The words hit her like a strong gust of wind. She felt like she was on her toes, almost lifting off her feet.

She reached out and touched his arm. "Maddox..."

He didn't turn toward her. He just stared into the shadows

65

beneath the bleachers.

Twilight had gone and darkness had fallen. She could barely see him in the dim light that seeped from the arena.

"The truth is, everyone around here thinks I finished my degree, but I'm a year short. The only reason the principal offered me that job is he thinks I've got a piece of paper with my name on it. But I don't."

She knew about a man's pride. Her own father had chased jobs across the nation, wanting to *provide* for his girl. She could only imagine how having to admit something like this was hitting Maddox.

"Without a college education, jobs like working on the harvest crew are all I've got. With Justin out of commission and medical bills piling up...if the price of cattle falls any more, we'll be butchering our own. Working is all I know how to do. It's all I'm good for."

She grabbed his arm and yanked until he rounded on her.

She looked up at him with all the love swelling in her heart and into her throat, making it impossible to speak. She swallowed and forced the words out.

"No, it's not," she whispered. "No, it's *not*."

She slid her hands behind his neck and tugged him down toward her.

He seemed to understand. His lips slanted over hers, his hands slipped around her waist, and if he held her just a little too tightly, well, that was okay with her.

A loudspeaker squealed, breaking the moment. She backed away a step, touched her lips with a trembling hand. A disembodied voice announced the start of the bull riding.

Looking down, she saw both of their hats had fallen into the dust.

She bent to pick them up and offered his to him. He took it, but she didn't let go. Their eyes met and connected over the top.

"I don't know what's gonna happen," he said in a low voice.

Neither did she. She didn't know how long Aunt Matilda would hold on, or how Livy's ice cream business would do.

Or if she'd walk away at the end of all of this with her heart intact.

But she couldn't walk away from Maddox right now.

She entwined her fingers with his and tugged him back up into the stands.

CHAPTER EIGHT

It was over.

Aunt Matilda was gone.

Haley sat through the funeral on the first pew in the little country church. Numb.

She and her aunt had made most of the arrangements in advance, so there had only been a few things to take care of, although she'd spent the last two days in a sea of paperwork, insurance claims, and lawyers.

How could it be that Haley would never see Aunt Matilda again? That her closest family member was lost to her?

Tears spilled over again, and Haley bowed her head, covered her face with her hands, and let them come.

She missed her. If only she'd made more time to come home since she'd left for college.

She'd always thought *there's time*.

And now, there was no time left.

A warm, wide hand rested on the center of her back. Maddox.

They were seated so close, she could feel the heat of his thigh next to hers. He'd been a steady presence the last couple of days. Bringing her food when she'd forgotten to eat. Answering the door to the church ladies when Haley couldn't face their kindness for her grief. He'd answered his phone in the wee hours when she couldn't sleep.

Olivia and Justin had been in and out, tiptoeing around and whispering like she was fine china. But this wasn't going to break her.

If she'd learned anything this summer, it was that cowgirls got back up after they got bucked off. And they didn't let go of what was important.

She was in love with Maddox.

She hadn't figured out how she was going to make it work between them. She had a job, back in Oklahoma City. Her boss had granted her another few days of leave to wrap things up, but he expected her back soon.

And Maddox was very firmly entrenched in Redbud Trails. He wasn't letting go of the farm without a fight. And he shouldn't. It was their family legacy, the place where Katie had grown up and Olivia could connect with her mother.

Everything was a muddle.

But today, all Haley could do was grieve. With Maddox beside her, holding her up, she could let Aunt Matilda go.

She would wait for a chance to talk to Maddox later.

A week later, Haley was still waiting.

Maddox had had to leave for the harvest crew the day after the funeral. The four-day separation had distanced them. He'd come home quieter, more reserved. She didn't know how to get their closeness back.

This morning, he'd come to help her load her car. It hadn't taken long, and now as he stowed the last of her boxes in the trunk, she stood in the empty dining room.

Out the window, a *For Sale* sign out front was the tangible sign that nothing would ever be the same.

She hesitated inside the front door, looking at Maddox's broad shoulders as he waited by her car.

What if... what if she'd been wrong about his feelings? For several days, she'd been mired in grief. All the insurance paperwork had kept her busy, slightly on edge, and frustrated.

And now Maddox was back, and that insidious voice in her head—a voice that sounded remarkably like Paul's—kept reminding her that she *wasn't enough*. She had never been enough to keep her father from chasing the next best job. Paul had found her wanting—criticizing her because she wasn't outgoing enough, telling her she needed to be a perfect hostess when they eventually got married.

What if...what if Maddox found her wanting as well?

Steeling herself with a deep breath, she stepped outside her aunt's door, trying not to think about how it was the last time she would, and locked it behind her.

His hands rested casually in his front pockets. His Stetson threw a shadow over his eyes, and she couldn't read them. His body language was casual, friendly.

But not welcoming.

She stopped several feet away, keys jangling in her nerveless fingers.

"Well, that's it," she said on an exhale.

If he would just give her an indication that he felt the same way he had when he'd kissed her before, at the rodeo...

But he only nodded, unsmiling.

"I'm not ready," she said softly. "To say goodbye." To the house, to her aunt's memory.

But especially to him.

Maddox fisted his hands in his jeans pockets, the muscles in his arms aching from wanting to reach for her.

He kept his jaw clenched to hold back the tide. Words like, *please don't leave me*. Words like, *I love you*.

She deserved better than a cowboy who was fighting for every paycheck.

His dad had given up, failed the family, nearly lost the farm.

But Maddox refused to do the same. Even if he was one overdue mortgage payment away from losing the place, he couldn't give up.

And that meant a lot of hard work.

How could he commit to—how could he ask Haley to commit to—a long-distance relationship when he knew he couldn't commit to it himself? He couldn't. His focus had to be on keeping his family afloat.

He'd watched his mother get beaten down by life and a husband who'd ultimately failed the family. He couldn't ask

Haley to do the same.

Or worse, start a relationship with her and a year down the road, have her decide to ditch the loser who was still working his butt off for a chunk of land.

He'd die if she walked away from him. He felt about like he was dying now. Like a big ol' bull had stepped on his chest cavity.

The best he could hope for was in a few months to have made some good money, put another nest egg aside, and when he'd proved he could support his family, call her. With any luck, she wouldn't fall in love with someone else.

All those words settled in his heart, tucked away. "Drive safe." He didn't add, *call me when you get there* or *I'll miss you.*

He couldn't bear the uncertainty in her eyes, so he turned away, yanking open her car door. She slipped under his arm, silent. Watchful. Waiting.

But he couldn't give her what she needed, so he said nothing.

And she started the car and drove away.

CHAPTER NINE

"Hello?"

"Is this Maddox Michaels?"

"Speaking. Who's this?"

"Dan Crane."

Hearing the junior high principal's voice on the phone pulled Maddox up short. He was on a three-day weekend back from the harvest crew, driving to town to make Olivia's weekly ice cream delivery to the restaurant that acted as a consignment agent for her, but now he stopped his truck on the side of the state highway.

"Dan. I've been meaning to return your calls."

He took a deep breath and decided to come clean.

"Actually, I haven't," he said. "Been meaning to call."

"Look, Maddox, we need you. There's no one else around qualified to coach—"

"I'm not qualified to teach," he said. And that shut the other man up. "I never finished my degree. I was a year short. I let everybody around here think I was done because I was too chicken to admit I was so much like my father."

His free hand clenched the bottom of the steering wheel.

There was a beat of silence before Dan spoke. "I wish I'd known this sooner."

Yeah. No kidding.

More silence and Maddox wanted to get out of the uncomfortable conversation. "I'll let you go—"

"Hang on a minute, Michaels. I'm thinking. You know, if we can get you enrolled..."

"What?"

While Maddox listened in shock, the other man outlined a plan for Maddox to finish his degree and get certified to teach—by Christmastime.

He wasn't even sure what he'd agreed to by the time the call ended twenty minutes later, but he did know that in one phone conversation, hope had come back to him.

But having a job didn't make up for losing Haley.

Every time he breathed in deeply, it felt like knives slicing through his lungs. He missed her so much.

It had been almost three weeks, and he'd heard nothing. Not that he'd expected to—he'd made his wishes clear that last day. But now, he was dying inside, a little each day.

He was still mulling the new job offer over when he got home with the boxed meal the restaurant manager had pushed on him.

Only to find Justin on his feet, wrestling with the old brown recliner.

"What're you doing?" Maddox dumped the food on the kitchen table and rushed to take the weight of the chair. Last thing Justin needed was for that chair to topple over and land on his only remaining good leg.

"I got to thinking," Justin said, huffing. "That it's time to get rid of this old thing."

Their eyes met over the top of the stinky chair.

He knew what Justin was saying. More than the recliner, it was time to let the past go.

His dad had sat in the chair and drunk himself to death. Maddox barely had any good memories of the man.

Ma had sat in this chair, swallowed by her grief. After she'd lost Katie, she'd lost herself.

Justin had almost done the same. His injury had made him give up on life.

But if he was man enough to get out of the chair, he was on the road to total recovery. His hip might not be fully functional, and he might always have a limp, but he could move on.

Maddox felt a hot burn behind his eyes. He cleared his throat. "I'm proud of you."

"Yeah, yeah." Justin leaned down to pick up the crutch he'd laid across the fireplace hearth. "After you take that out to the dump, you need to get in your truck and head to Oklahoma City."

Maddox grunted. He angled the chair toward the door, eyeing the frame. The chair wasn't going to fit upright.

"I'm not kidding," Justin said. "You can't just let a girl like Haley get away."

Maddox pushed the chair across the floor. It hung up on a patch of old carpet and he almost fell over the top of it, getting a good wallop in the stomach when it rebounded.

"Mad. I'm serious."

"She's the one who left," he huffed. She'd left him behind. Again.

"And you've been moping around here for three weeks. You've got two feet and a truck. So go get her and bring her back."

His heart panged once, hard. "It's not that easy. I've got a lead on a job, but I've got to prove myself—"

"Prove what?" Justin demanded. "Prove that you're just as much of an idiot as our father? She's in love with you—if you haven't messed that up. She'll stand by you."

He wanted to believe...wanted to believe it so badly.

Maddox's heart thudded in his chest. "I've been pretty stupid."

"No kidding. What else is new? But she fell in love with you knowing that football players have a couple screws loose, so this little act of stupidity probably hasn't surprised her much."

Could he really take Justin's advice?

What if she couldn't forgive him for breaking her heart?

Worse than that, what if he never tried to put it back together?

Haley had settled into her normal routine.

Sort of.

She went to work. And stared at her computer screen all day. She wasn't getting a lot done.

She came home. And tried not to stare at her phone, willing Maddox to call.

She'd called his house and spoken to Livy several times, checking on the business, checking on the girl.

She'd shied away from asking about Maddox. When Livy had offered tidbits like *he liked the root beer float flavor*, Haley had *mm-hmmed* and moved on.

What was wrong with her?

She had a car. Gas. Keys. She could drive back to Redbud Trails any time. She wanted to take the man by the shoulders and shake him. Or maybe kiss him.

She didn't know what she'd been thinking that last day. Maybe she'd let her grief blind her, or her fear.

She *knew* there was something between her and Maddox. It had been too strong to deny, and too strong to fade away.

She'd talked herself into a weekend trip and had her keys dangling from her fingers when she exited her front door. And stopped short.

There was a big, dusty truck in her driveway.

She barely registered the truck before a tall, dusty cowboy stood in her way, too.

She threw herself at him. And he caught her.

"What took you so long?" she mumbled into his shoulder.

He rumbled a laugh. "Sorry." She felt the press of his chin in her hair. "It took this big, dumb *Ox* a little bit to get things figured out."

She tilted her chin back and squinted up at him. "Don't call yourself dumb."

He used the opportunity to rub his thumb along the line of her jaw.

"So what did you figure out?" she whispered.

"Well, the financial situation is still a little sticky," he said. "But mostly, I realized that I was focusing on the wrong things, like your dad did."

He brushed a kiss across her temple.

"And letting the best thing in my life get away, kind of like my dad did."

Now he brushed a kiss across her cheek.

"And I don't want to be like either of them."

"You're not—" she started to say.

And he sure kissed her like he agreed.

When they broke away minutes later, both panting and out-of-breath, he noticed the keys dangling from her hand. "Going somewhere?"

"I was on my way to Redbud Trails." She couldn't help the shy smile. "You're not the only one who was being less-smart than they should be." She looked down briefly but then back up at him, his overwhelming presence—and his kisses—giving her courage. "I shouldn't have left without telling you I was in love with you."

He lit up from the inside out.

"And not because of your bank account," she went on. "Or your farm."

He lifted his eyebrows.

"It's definitely because of your niece's ice cream." She stood on her tiptoes and brushed a kiss against his lips. "I want a piece of the business."

He leaned down and kissed her beneath her jaw. "You already own a piece of it."

"Hmm." She giggled and tucked her chin down when his hot breath tickled her neck. "I guess it must be something else, then."

She pushed on his shoulders until he was far enough away that she could see his face. "It's because of who you are. The man who wouldn't give up on his brother. Who redid the kitchen to make a little girl's dream come true."

The quiet joy on his face made the heartfelt confession easy.

"Wanna know why I'm in love with you?" he asked.

Her heart soared up into her throat, and she nodded.

He cupped her jaw in one hand. "Same reason. Because of who you are. Your quiet spirit and gentle heart that saw my niece's needs and found a way to meet them. You reached out to Justin when the rest of the outside world forgot him and gave him the courage to go on." He swallowed hard. "And you found a way inside my heart when I thought it was too full of worrying about everything else." His expression darkened. "I don't know how everything's going to work out."

"That's okay. We can figure it out together."

"Together." He breathed in deeply. "That sounds so right."

And he kissed her again.

LOVE LETTERS FROM COWBOY

PROLOGUE

She was alive.

Ryan Michaels repeated the refrain mentally as he stood on the threshold of Ashley's room at Walter Reed. Behind him and standing beside the nurse's desk, the military doctor was updating Mrs. Reynolds, Ashley's mom, on her condition. Ryan could hear the low rumble of the man's voice, but he couldn't make out the words.

Ryan couldn't wait any longer to see the woman he loved. No matter what she looked like, or what she'd lost, she was alive. That's what mattered right now. When she was less critical, he was sure there would be adjustments. A lot of them.

He held his breath as he stepped over the threshold and approached the hospital bed.

The room was dark except for soft, under-counter lighting along one wall. He let his eyes adjust. It smelled sanitary, like a hospital should, but the antiseptic scent burned his nostrils. He wished he were home, out in the pasture, smelling the sweet alfalfa.

And that she were with him.

There was no sound of welcome, just the soft swish and beep from the plethora of machines surrounding her bed.

Her face was exposed, but most everything else was covered in bandages. Her eyes were closed, her lashes dark fans against her pale cheeks. She looked like a ghost of the summer-tanned Ashley he remembered.

Was she sleeping? The doctor had told Ashley's mom she'd been in and out of consciousness, that she was aware of her injury. He supposed she'd been lucky when that roadside bomb exploded and overturned the transport she'd been riding in. She'd lost an arm, but she was still alive.

He burned, knowing that no one she loved had been beside her when she'd found that out. He could've taken a red-eye and been here sooner, but her mom was still a little fragile after the mild heart attack she'd suffered three weeks ago, and he'd wanted to help Mary navigate the unfamiliar Baltimore airport and ease what stress he could.

Had Ashley cried? He couldn't picture it, not when he knew how stoic Ashley tended to be when she got bad news—really, when anything hurt her.

"Oh, Ash," he sighed as he came near her bedside.

Her lashes fluttered, and her eyes opened. She looked at him with those intense blue irises that he would never forget.

"Am I dreaming? You never call me that..."

Because she would always be Ashley to him.

Her voice was a rough whisper. He'd been warned it would take awhile to return after they removed the ventilator. *~only hand?*

He couldn't resist. He clasped her good hand in his, noting how small and cool it was against his rough farmer's mitt. She didn't pull away. She was either willing to accept his comfort or too tired or hurt to move away.

She licked her lips. They looked dry and cracked, and he made a mental note to talk to her nurse about getting some lip balm.

"What are you doing here?" she asked, again in that terrible whisper.

He hesitated. How much did she know about how things were at home? He'd written her the truth in his letters, but he didn't know if she'd actually read them. If she didn't know about her mom's condition, he wasn't going to tell her now, not like this.

"Your mom needed a travel buddy." He nodded toward the hall. "She's still talking to the doctor." He hoped it was enough explanation. As soon as Ashley saw her mom, she'd know that something wasn't right.

But she didn't need to worry about that now. The doctor had said there was still a chance of infection, and Ryan didn't want her worrying about things that couldn't be changed. He just wanted her well.

"So you... came to annoy me... into getting better?"

"Whatever it takes, Sweet-Pea." He crooked a smile at her.

"You look... terrible."

He glanced down at himself. The Wrangler jeans had seen better days. He'd slept in his T-shirt on the plane, and his chin desperately needed a razor. She was probably right.

His chin still tucked down, he grinned up at her. "You look too beautiful for words." It was true. Even beat up and covered in gauze bandages, she was a sight he never wanted to forget. Before she could protest, he rushed on, "You want a drink?"

He helped her take a few sips of water, careful not to lean on the bed, afraid of hurting her.

"Can you... check on Atlas?"

For a moment he had no idea what she was talking about. And then it hit him. Her dog. Her Military Working Dog. Her partner.

Had they been out on an assignment together? If Ashley had almost died, was there a chance the dog had survived?

Thinking about how close he'd come to losing her brought a hot thickness to his throat. "I'll find out."

Her eyelids fluttered closed, and he took her hand again. More for him than for her, this time.

He'd come here to offer support for her mom. He'd thought, after Ashley had been away so long, after she'd never answered one of his letters, that the distance had diminished his feelings for her.

He'd been wrong.

Seeing her like this was a wakeup call.

He still loved her. He'd known it when she was sixteen and he fourteen. He knew it now as a twenty-six year old man, deep in his gut and reverberating throughout his body.

There was never going to be anybody else for him.

When she got through this, when she was back home in Redbud Trails, Oklahoma, back on her feet and re-building her confidence, as no doubt she would need to, that's when he would make one thousand percent sure she knew about his feelings.

He would woo her.

He would prove he was the man for her.

He would make her fall in love with him, too.

CHAPTER ONE

Six weeks later

Ash Reynolds released both her white-knuckled grip and the breath she'd been holding as the plane touched down and slowed to ground speed.

She didn't mind flying. Had been all over the world as part of her military career. But she hated landing.

"All right, boy?" she asked her flying companion.

Atlas, the huge German Shepherd Dog lying at her feet glanced up, panting. One of his ears cocked to beautiful attention. The other was only half-there, a visible reminder of the terror they'd survived. Just like her empty shirt-sleeve.

She was looking forward to her homecoming today. And she was dreading it. She wanted to see her parents. Her mom had been there in the early days after Ash's amputation and had told her it was time to come home. Her dad's Alzheimer's was getting worse, and they needed Ash.

She needed the direction. But things with her parents were...difficult.

After high school graduation, Ashley had found out the truth. She'd been adopted as an infant. The fact that her parents hadn't told her after a lifetime of opportunity had broken her heart. How could they keep something so important from her?

Over several months, that hurt had festered until she had seriously questioned her identity. Who was she, really?

She'd found herself in the Marines. As a soldier, as a MWD handler. She and her partner, Atlas, had been responsible for saving countless lives.

And now she'd not just lost an arm, she'd lost that identity—Ashley the soldier.

Her parents needed her. Maybe she could help in the family feed store.

Was that who Ashley was now? Small-town girl.

The moniker fit like a coat two sizes too small.

And...

Everything would be different now.

Everyone in Redbud Trails—people she had known all her life would *look at her*. And have questions. She dreaded the questions.

She'd started to come to terms with her condition. Her handicap. She was an amputee.

It didn't mean she was less of a woman. She just had to work harder to do certain things than the two-armed population.

Sometimes, in the dead of night when she couldn't sleep, when the arm that wasn't there anymore *ached*, she got a little bitter about it. Why had this happened to her? Why did she have to fight so hard for *everything*? As a child, she'd worked so hard to fit in, not knowing why it felt so difficult. As a soldier, she'd struggled to get her counterparts to accept her in a male-dominated field. Then, for survival. And now, sometimes just getting through the day was a battle.

It was a battle she would fight, though. And win. She was no quitter.

She just had to figure out what to do with her life now. Before her injury, she'd thought she would be career military. That dream had disappeared with her arm. In combat situations, her amputation prevented her from both carrying a weapon and controlling her dog—and she refused to put her partner in danger. So here she was.

Back home, where everything had started.

She and Atlas were on the emergency exit row, so he'd have more room at her feet. As a MWD, he was allowed in the cabin. But he was retired now, like her. Discharged because he'd lost hearing in his injured ear.

At least she'd been allowed to keep him. He'd been a big part of her life for the last several years. They'd trained together, been at war together. Those kinds of things bonded you. And... almost dying together? They were linked, that was for sure.

The seatbelt light blinked off, and it took twice as long to unbuckle her belt with only one hand to release the mechanism. She stood, and took care to settle her carryon bag over her shoulder and adjust the strap before she picked up Atlas's leash and moved into the aisle. If it started to ride down her arm, she would have to completely stop and settle the dog before she could fix it. Limitations.

In the terminal, passengers streamed along in an unchoreographed dance. Businessmen in suits with rolling luggage. Soccer moms trying to corral their kids. Young people with backpacks slung over their shoulders. None paying a bit of attention to the returning veteran.

Until Ashley stepped out of the secured passenger area and into the public terminal. A crowd had gathered around. Several people were waving flags. She wasn't three feet beyond security when they started clapping and whistling. Her face flared hot. Her hand tensed on Atlas's leash, and he looked back at her, waiting for instructions, just like always. Asking her with those warm brown eyes if this was a situation they needed to control.

She reassured him with a smile. This wasn't dangerous—not in the way he understood danger, anyway.

In front of the crowd was a tall figure holding a handmade sign written on poster board that read, "Welcome home, Ashley" and was signed "Love, Cowboy." Her heart sped up for one intense moment. But the incorrigible grin and dancing eyes beneath his brown Stetson made it hard to believe anything Ryan Michaels said—or wrote.

She spared a thought for the packet of letters she'd tied with a ribbon and stowed at the bottom of her bag. Unopened.

She should've known he was behind this fanfare. Her parents never would've done something like this.

Her feet moved toward him on autopilot, Atlas at her side. She was still scanning the gathered crowd for her parents when she reached him.

"Where are Mom and Dad?" She almost had to shout to be heard over the still-applauding group.

A shadow shifted behind his expressive brown eyes. Blond curls peeked from beneath his hat. "They sent me to get you."

It wasn't the whole story. But maybe now wasn't the time to push for answers, not with all these people watching.

And chanting.

Chanting?

It started low, with only one or two voices calling out, but then the crowd picked up the refrain and the hum became audible.

"Kiss her! Kiss her!"

Ash's face flamed even hotter—burning like the hot sands in the desert where she'd been stationed.

"Don't you dare," she growled at Ryan.

The shouting might've drowned out her voice, but she would bet he could read her lips. He grinned and shrugged, affecting a *what can you do?* air. He stepped closer, and Atlas looked up at her again, probably confused by her uncertain body language.

She used a hand command to make the dog sit but the moment of lost focus meant that Ryan was that much closer when she looked back up at him.

"Kiss her! Kiss her!"

His hands came to rest gently on her hips. She held up her arm to fend him off, lips parted to protest, and that's when he did it.

Kissed her.

Right there in public.

His lips were cool, and she felt the very faint scrape of stubble when his chin rubbed against hers. His Stetson brushed the top of her hair, and he smelled so good—like man and leather and cowboy...

He smelled so good that for a moment, she got lost in the

kiss. Somehow her hand tangled up in his shirt—she hadn't really clenched her fist to hold him there, had she?

And then he was looking down on her, his brown eyes dancing.

Though she couldn't hear him over the cheers and wolf whistles of the crowd, she saw his lips move. *"You wanna get out of here?"*

The military had trained her to make quick decisions. Working with Atlas on missions where discovering explosive devices happened too often to count, sometimes she had only a fraction of a second to decide a course of action. The way she saw it, she could pay a very large sum of money to take a taxi back to Redbud Trails—if she could even find one that would drive that far. Or she could ride back with the man who'd just knocked her socks off with that kiss.

If she had had cash on her, she would've opted for the taxi.

As it was, she sighed and muttered an assent.

Ashley had steamed him up with that kiss.

She'd *kissed him back*.

And judging by the way she was marching ahead of him toward the baggage claim, she was steamed *at* him. At least she'd been polite to the assembled crowd, shaking hands and accepting well wishes before the small group had dispersed.

"I didn't tell them to say that," he told her.

She iced him with a glare.

"That's not how I pictured our first kiss," he tried.

Now her expression turned incredulous, and he hastened to explain. "I mean, I have thought about it a few times..."

She shook her head, a cute blush on her cheeks. "You always did have a crazy imagination."

"So when can we do it again?"

Her glare came back, but he laughed. He was thrilled that she was finally here. He'd been planning this homecoming for a week, ever since her mom had told him about it. It couldn't have gone better, not in any of the dozen ways he'd imagined it.

"Let me take your bag," he said.

She kept juggling the leash and her duffel, without a second hand to help her adjust. "I've got it."

Well, maybe in his imagination, she'd been a little happier to see him.

"Really, I'd like to carry it for you."

"Really, I've got it." She sighed. "I've got some checked luggage, though. You can get a cart." Her grudging allowance maybe wasn't all he'd been looking for, but he had a two-hour drive with her in the cab of his truck. And a couple of surprises up his sleeve.

He loaded her huge suitcase and two good-sized boxes onto a cart and pushed it through the sliding doors into the sultry, Oklahoma summer air. It was only beginning of May, but temperatures had hit the nineties yesterday, and today looked to be the same.

She walked slightly behind him, the dog between them, and he heard her huff of surprise as she crossed the threshold out of the air conditioning and into the outdoors.

"How was your flight from San Antone?" he asked conversationally. He knew she'd gone back to an on-base apartment after the military hospital had released her.

She grunted.

Maybe if he tried another tack...

"Your mom and dad are really excited to see you," he said. "But I have some bad news."

He waited until she looked up at him.

"They're throwing you a welcome home party. It's supposed to be a surprise, but I know how much you like those, so I thought I'd give you a warning now."

He was rambling. That's how excited he was. He was like a little puppy, tail wagging and begging her to love him.

Love him back.

She hadn't even commented on his sign. Had she recognized the reference to how he'd signed the dozens of letters he'd sent her while she'd been stationed overseas?

She looked at him askance. "You're kidding, right?"

He shook his head. "Sorry, Sweet-Pea. They've invited pretty much the whole town. Closing the store an hour early. Food. Big banner. You're the guest of honor."

She groaned, and her dog's ears—both the good one and the one that was only half-there—stood at attention.

She made some kind of *kssh* noise in her throat and the dog relaxed again. If just a little groan could get that kind of reaction from the dog, what must it look like facing a real threat? More importantly, how had the dog learned to read her so well?

She and the dog were *that* attuned to each other.

Ryan was a little jealous.

He nodded to his truck, glad he'd parked in the more expensive terminal lot so she didn't have to walk quite so far in the oppressive heat.

"You're still driving this old rust-bucket?" she asked incredulously.

"It's a Ford," he said. A little defensively. "They last a lifetime. Or so." He patted the side of the truck comfortingly.

She made a funny face at him.

But that's just the kind of guy he was. He drove the same truck for ten years. Worked at the same job he'd had in high school—although with vastly different responsibilities now. Loved the same woman for a good twelve years.

Yeah, he was a little stubborn.

Her dog was standing stiffly, nose pointed up slightly, and Ashley looked like she might be inclined to back away.

"What's the matter?"

"Atlas got a hit on your truck," she said, like he ought to know what that meant. "Do you have something illegal in there? Drugs, bomb-making supplies?"

She looked so serious that he laughed. "Real funny."

"Look at him." She jerked her chin toward the dog. "He smells something."

"Yeah, something good." Ryan reached over the side of the truck bed and pulled out a plastic bag he'd tucked down there.

Ashley looked like she wanted to bolt, but her eyes were

glued to his hands as he unwrapped... a couple of foil-wrapped treats.

"They're pumpkin dog biscuits—basically pumpkin and molasses," he told her, crouching down to the dog's level and offering one on the flat of his hand.

The dog looked back at her, its tail wagging a slow *whuff* through the air.

She still looked skeptical.

"I baked them myself."

She nodded to the dog, who zoomed forward and took the thing before Ryan had even registered the slide of its tongue across his palm.

"Thought I might need a bribe for your partner here."

When he tilted his head back so he could get a clear view of her face without the brim of his Stetson in his way, she was looking at him like he'd told her he was an alien from another planet.

Like she didn't understand him at all.

Maybe she never had.

He gave the second biscuit to the dog, who snarfed it down in two bites. Ryan stood up, wiping his hands on his jeans.

Ashley was looking into the truck bed, eyes focused on the extra-large dog crate he'd borrowed from the store. He'd secured it in the back of the truck with numerous industrial-strength bungee cords.

Then she looked back at him like she still couldn't figure him out. Her eyes narrowed in on his chest.

"Are you wearing...?" She started to say something, and then her voice faded out. "You don't still...?"

"Work for your parents?" he finished for her. He'd left directly from work and hadn't changed out of his T-shirt that bore the logo for the feed store. Did she really not know? He was surprised her parents hadn't mentioned him—or maybe Ashley had steered the conversation away from him if it ever came up.

Her expression turned chagrined, like she was embarrassed she'd asked or embarrassed *for* him, but he wasn't ashamed of it.

"Did you read *any* of my letters?" he asked.

"What letters?" She said the words flippantly, and for a moment, he wondered if something had gone wrong and somehow he'd sent all those letters to someone else.

But her hand tightened on the leash, her knuckles flashing white.

Why would she lie? Maybe she didn't want to talk about it right now.

"I do still work at the feed store," he said. He worked to keep his voice easy and his expression mellow—he wasn't looking to scare her off by pushing too hard. "I'm the manager now."

"Hmm."

Oh, that sound! Like she had something else to say. "What?" he asked.

"I thought... seems like I heard you'd dropped out of college, too."

This time he had to work to make himself sound easy and relaxed. Not to grind his back teeth. "I guess not everybody's cut out be a traditional student."

She hadn't really asked a question, and he didn't correct her.

Maybe she really hadn't gotten his letters. In them, he'd told her all about switching from a full-time student to a non-traditional night student, taking only part time classes. Back when her dad had started having a hard time keeping things straight at the store.

Was that really how she saw him? A deadbeat in the same job he'd had since high school, a college dropout?

If so, he didn't sound like the kind of guy that would attract someone as smart and well-traveled as Ashley. If he was going to win her, he had his work cut out for him.

And how was he going to tell her everything he'd done for her family while she'd been overseas? He sure wasn't about to go bragging. But she was a smart cookie.

Once she started seeing things around the feed store, she'd understand. He hoped.

And then what about her parents' farmland? Would she understand why he'd leased it? That was another situation entirely, separate from the feed store. Maybe he'd better wait to bring it up.

"You want the dog in the back or up front?" he asked.

She looked at him with her eyes somewhat narrowed. Maybe he'd surprised her in some way by not arguing or being embarrassed about who he was. He didn't know.

"It's pretty hot out. He'd probably prefer the A/C," she murmured.

Ryan shrugged. "Fine by me. Means you'll have to sit in the center. Next to me," he added, in case she didn't get what he meant.

He quickly loaded up her boxes and bags, securing the whole thing with a few more ties, since they'd be on the interstate.

She and the dog were already in the cab when he got back from returning the luggage cart, and it wasn't Ashley's sweet-smelling breath that hit him in the face when he slid into the driver's seat.

The huge shepherd sat in the middle seat. On his haunches, he was easily as tall as Ryan seated. And although he panted in an easy doggie smile, it wasn't exactly who Ryan wanted to snuggle up to.

Ryan leaned around the dog to shoot her a disbelieving look.

She smiled a ghost of a smile.

Ah well. Maybe winning her smile was worth sitting next to the monster of a dog all the way back to Redbud Trails. As long as it didn't bite.

Ryan had to be the most easygoing person alive.

It irritated the snot out of Ashley.

She was hot and sticky from the walk out to his truck—although the icy air blasting in her face was helping with that—and though she hated to admit it, she was still flustered from his impromptu kiss.

Aside from that moment when he asked if she wanted something to eat—she didn't—they were both quiet as he navigated the city traffic. He tuned the radio to a country station, and she found herself relaxing. Which was dangerous. She didn't know what to expect from this grown-up Ryan.

In high school, he'd asked her out all the time. It had been a running joke between them. She'd always said *no*. The one time she'd actually contemplated going on a date with him, she'd dismissed the idea. He was two years her junior. He'd been immature. She'd been thinking about college and her future, then blasted by the news of her adoption.

It had all been a joke. Right?

After they'd made it out of the city and the traffic had spread out some, he stretched one arm across the back of the seats, his fingertips brushing her shoulder and sending a cascade of sparks down her spine. She threaded her fingers into Atlas's fur.

"So you said you wanted to talk to me. Is there something going on with my parents?" Or had the warning about the surprise welcome home party been his only motivation for coming? With Ryan, she never knew. Back in high school, he'd always been the jokester.

He tapped his fingers on the seatback, and they brushed against her again. She straightened her spine, hoping to put some centimeters between her shoulder and his touch.

"I just wanted to explain that things have changed around the store, are different than you might remember."

"How so?"

"Lots of things. New timecard scanning system and computerized—"

Atlas must've decided he'd had enough of sitting, because he lay down with am exhaled *whuff*. He was so big that his rear pushed into Ashley's thigh, and he set his paws into Ryan's lap and rested his head on top of them.

She'd never seen anything like it. Atlas was *her dog*. She'd trained him since he'd come into the program. He'd never had another trainer and had never really responded to others, though he would occasionally accept affection from some of the soldiers where they'd been stationed overseas. He bore it more for their sake than for his own.

He'd *never* rested on someone else's lap before. What had Ryan put in those dog treats?

Ryan looked a little unsure about having the dog so close.

"I'll make him sit up," she offered.

Atlas cocked one ear, like he knew they were talking about him, but otherwise he didn't move. Traitor.

"He's fine, I guess. Long as he doesn't bump the steering wheel."

She'd been surprised that Ryan had thought about putting a crate for Atlas in the truck. Some irresponsible people might've just put a dog loose in the truck bed—which was a recipe for disaster as the animal could get hurt or killed—but Ryan had thought to secure the crate, and she'd even seen a cushion when she'd glanced inside it. And he hadn't balked at all when she'd suggested Atlas sit in the cab.

She didn't want to think about him making special overtures for her dog.

"You were saying something about computers," she reminded him in a murmur.

"Yeah. Your pops put in a POS—point-of-sale system. It's easier on the cashier and has the inventory right on the computer—"

"My *dad* put in a computer thing?"

Interestingly, pink crept up into Ryan's neck and bled into his cheeks. Was he blushing? "All right, it might not have been your dad's idea, but having the records on computer has been much easier. Even he would tell you so."

"Whose idea was it?"

"Ah. Mine." He seemed uncomfortable admitting to it. The question was *why?*

"So you're the manager now, and you've installed some new systems. What else?"

He shifted his shoulders—his hand along the back of the seat bumped her back. "Your dad doesn't spend as much time in the store. It's been hard for him. He's probably a lot different than you remember, too."

She swallowed hard. "His Alzheimer's?"

Ryan nodded. Serious, for once.

Guilt panged. She hadn't made as many visits home as she could've. When she'd had leave, she'd often used the excuse of needing to care for Atlas to stay at Lackland.

Her parents had been older than many of her friends' parents. It hadn't made sense when she'd been a kid, but when she found out she'd been adopted, it all became clear. They'd been in their fifties already when she was a teenager. And now... her dad was slipping away.

"Your mom was bringing him to the store more, but after her attack, she's been staying home more and more."

Ashley's heart stuttered. "What attack?"

He glanced at her, brows down over his eyes like he was puzzled. "You really didn't read my letters. Your mom didn't tell you when she was down at the hospital after...your arm??"

Her mom had stayed with her through those first agonizing weeks of pain. Ashley had been in and out of consciousness. She could barely remember those days.

And every once in awhile, she remembered the vivid dreams she'd had, that *Ryan* had come to her in the hospital.

Which was ridiculous, of course. Why would he have?

And although he sometimes joked about loving her, like he had with his poster board sign back in the terminal, he didn't really think about her like that.

It must've been the strong pain medications they'd been giving her.

Ryan was silent as he pulled off the highway at an exit in the middle of nowhere. One lonely gas station interrupted the flat landscape. He pulled the truck into the parking lot, far from both the pumps and the tiny store, and shoved it into park.

Ashley's heart thundered in her ears. Had something happened to her mom and no one had told her about it?

Ryan shifted, turned toward her a little bit. Atlas groaned at the insult of being moved out of his comfortable position, but he raised his head as Ryan did. Ryan moved his palm to cup her shoulder and she braced herself.

"Your mom had a mild heart attack in early March."

Three weeks before Ashley's near-fatal run in with terrorists. The information bomb burst with painful accuracy in her stomach and sent shards of pain through her.

Ashley could barely breathe through the tightness in her chest. "And no one told me?"

He shook his head, those brown eyes filled with compassion until she couldn't look at him. She turned her face to the window, not really seeing what was outside. Her eyes burned, but she didn't cry. She never cried.

Ryan didn't move his hand from her shoulder. She should shrug off his comfort, but she didn't.

"Your dad... maybe he wasn't lucid enough to call. I don't know. Maybe your mom told him not to. Maybe she didn't want you to worry—she knew you were working in dangerous territory."

"Who took care of them?" she whispered.

But somehow, she knew what he was going to say before he said it.

"Your mom had been working in the flower bed outside— overexerting herself. That's what the doctor said—and her neighbor saw her fall. She called 9-1-1 and then called the store, and I came. Your dad was pretty shaken up. I sat with him at the hospital. And Pastor Philip came up and stayed the night with us."

And she hadn't been there.

"Why didn't you call me? Or send an email or something?" Her voice was shaking but the accusation was clear.

"I wrote it in the next letter I sent."

She shook her head. Whether she was denying the letters she'd never read or denying that he'd tried to do the right thing, she didn't know.

"You never did give me your phone number over there. Didn't feel right to snoop through your parents' things. I wasn't sure it was my place."

She blinked several times to clear the hot film from her eyes. Finally, she had calmed enough to turn back and smile tightly at him. Maybe now they could go. She wanted to be home, to see her parents for herself.

To be out of this truck. Away from Ryan.

"I'm surprised her doctors let her come to see me, only weeks after something like that."

Now he was looking at her funny again, forehead wrinkled. "They were concerned—that's why she had a travel buddy."

She went hot and cold as his words sank in. *Travel buddy.*

And then what she'd thought had been dreams or her imagination under medication and unbearable pain suddenly became very real.

Her eyes flew to his face. She shrugged off his hand out of pure self-preservation.

"You—?"

She couldn't finish, because she didn't know what she'd meant to say.

If he'd really been there, he'd...

He'd spent countless hours at her bedside while she'd sweated through phantom pains in her missing arm.

Read to her from a classic book, his voice soothing and low.

Told her funny stories from home, even though she'd been unable to muster a laugh.

And...

He'd seen her at her weakest.

She'd thought it couldn't have been real, but now, looking at his frown, she knew she was the one who'd made a mistake. A big one.

She'd underestimated him.

"Yeah," he said. "I was there."

"I thought I'd dreamed it," she whispered.

And felt a little like she was having a nightmare.

CHAPTER TWO

An hour after they'd pulled off the highway, Ryan delivered Ashley home.

She'd been quiet since his revelation in the truck. He wasn't sure how she'd forgotten that he'd been at her bedside all those weeks ago. She'd seemed lucid enough at the time, but maybe she'd been on more pain medication than he'd thought.

Or maybe she'd wanted to block it out.

He was feeling like his mission to make her fall in love with him had more roadblocks than he'd planned for.

But that was a problem for tomorrow. She was going to be seeing her parents and probably overwhelmed by the crowd. He'd do what he could to make it easier for her.

The Reynolds family lived in a two-story clapboard house in town as the farmland he leased didn't have a residence on it. He'd heard rumors that Joe had always meant to build out there but had put his business first and lived in town to be closer to the store.

Cars were parked in the drive, down the block, and around the corner. People spilled out the front door and onto the lawn. The big banner he'd hung across the front porch waved gently in the breeze. *Welcome home, Ash!*

When they pulled to a stop, the dog lifted its head off his lap. He hoped the animal had been comfortable, because he could feel the doggie-jaw sized moist spot on his thigh where, despite the A/C, he'd sweated through his jeans. He wouldn't have minded if it had been Ashley's warm skin against him. The dog just felt like a bad consolation prize.

Motionless, Ashley groaned.

"You'll be fine," he said. He stepped from the car and walked around to open her door, but she'd already wrangled it open by stretching her left arm across her body.

After a long, frightened gaze at the house, she looked up the street in one direction, then turned her head in the other. "Atlas probably needs to take a walk."

Was she thinking about bolting?

He heard a shout from inside the house. "Ashley's here!"

"She made it!"

Several people called out her name.

"I'll take him," Ryan offered, extending his hand for the leash.

She hesitated.

"You aren't going to have a chance." He heard the screen door open, and the voices got louder.

She turned toward the people streaming out of the house, then back to him with a terrified look on her face. Sure, improvised explosive devices in enemy territory, no problem. A crowd of old friends, and she looked like she wanted to run.

She relinquished the leash to him, and the dog followed him amiably enough to a neighbor's yard to do his business. Ryan craned his head over his shoulder, watching Ashley's friends envelope her in the crowd. Her blonde head bobbed among them as he watched her accept hugs and pats on the back.

Where was Mary, Ashley's mom? Probably in the kitchen, worried about being a good hostess.

The dog seemed uninterested in sniffing around, so Ryan left the crowded front yard behind. He took him around to the backyard and made sure there was a bowl of water and a patch of shade near the porch, then snuck in the back door. In the kitchen, Mary was frantically putting cold cuts on a serving platter.

"Hey, you," she said with a smile, but he noticed the flush high in her cheeks. She'd better not have over-taxed herself getting ready for the guests she'd invited this afternoon. Ashley would need her to be healthy.

He washed up at the sink. "Guest of honor is here. Why don't you let me finish up here and go hug your little girl?"

"You're a good boy," Mary said. She brushed the back of one hand across her forehead. "I think I'll take you up on that."

He was familiar with the kitchen that had been updated about a decade ago; he cooked for Ashley's parents a couple of times a week. It made things easier on them and it wasn't like he had a family waiting on him after he got home from work.

The Reynolds's house felt about like home to him. He'd grown to love the occasional squeak in the wood floors, the slip-covered furniture in the living room, the many childhood pictures of Ashley, the recliner that Joe inhabited beside the picture window where he could watch the birds.

He really hoped Ashley loved it here, wanted to stay. Her parents needed her. And he needed her too. She just didn't know it yet.

He finished arranging the meat and cheese platter and found some fruit she must've started chopping. He threw it on an empty plate too.

Then he took both platters out and put them on the overladen dining room table, greeting friends and nodding to his cousin Maddox across the room. He talked to several people before spotting Ashley. She was talking to a guy Ryan recognized from church. A single guy about his age who'd moved to town recently.

Who'd invited him?

The surge of hot jealousy took him by surprise. He'd already taken one step toward them but forced his feet to turn around. He went back to the kitchen instead. He didn't have a claim on Ashley, no matter how much he wished he did.

Ashley's dad, Joe, was standing with one hand on the back of one of the chairs in the breakfast nook, looking out the window into the backyard.

The kitchen door swung closed behind Ryan, muting the voices of the crowd in the other room. Joe looked back over his shoulder.

He looked tired. He'd aged in the last few years, added wrinkles and white hair. He'd been a steady presence in Ryan's life—not the father Ryan had never had, but certainly a mentor. Working with Joe had given Ryan direction, and Ryan liked to think they still would've been friends, even if Ryan hadn't been hung up on Ashley.

"Everything okay?" Ryan asked.

Joe shrugged. He looked at the door behind Ryan and then back outside. "I came in here after something, but for the life of me, I can't remember what it was."

That was pretty normal. So was Joe's frustration. As his memory failed, the things he couldn't remember seemed to increase daily and it was hard on him. Joe didn't particularly like crowds, because the people he knew from his memories had changed. It was confusing, upsetting. But Ashley deserved her party.

Ryan stood shoulder-to-shoulder with the older man. He wasn't needed at the party, not right now, when Ashley's attention was called a hundred different ways and everyone wanted to talk to her. But Joe needed him.

Even though he wanted to rush back into the party and pummel that guy from church. He'd seemed like a nice guy before today. Ryan's stomach hurt at the thought of Ashley falling for some other guy.

He'd had too many conversations with God about her to count. Ryan had thought he and the Big Guy were on the same page.

But what if he was wrong?

What if he'd wasted ten years of his life trying to win a girl who would never want him?

The sound of the party rose and fell, almost like someone had opened the door, but Ryan stayed with Joe and didn't look behind.

"How'd closing go tonight?" Joe asked.

"Moira closed," Ryan said gently. "I had to drive to Oklahoma City to pick up Ashley."

They'd talked about it last night when Ryan had been over for dinner, but it wasn't a huge surprise that Joe didn't remember.

"That's right," said the older man, rubbing the bridge of his nose between his finger and thumb.

"Did you get to talk to Ashley?"

"For a minute. Her friends were swarming around..." And sometimes Joe had trouble remembering names.

It was tough seeing the man who used to greet every customer at the feed store and not only remember their names, but the types and names of their horses and pets.

Joe squeezed the chair back and wiggled the chair a little, a sign of agitation. "I'd forgotten about...her arm. And her hair's shorter. She looks...different."

Ah. Maybe this was the real reason Joe had come to hide in the kitchen. His memories of Ashley had been from before her injury, and that blank in his memory must be painful, like finding out about her amputation all over again.

Ryan rested a hand on the older man's shoulder. "Mary said she put a recent picture of Ashley on your dresser," he said gently. "Would it help if we made a copy and put it on that little shelf next to your recliner?"

"Maybe." Joe stared out the back window.

"She's still the same Ash," Ryan said. "Independent and stubborn." *Prickly. Vulnerable.* "She wouldn't even let me open the car door for her."

"That sounds about right." Joe smiled a ghost of a smile. Ryan thought he'd better not mention the kiss. The old man was still protective of his daughter.

"She didn't even want to stop for food, she was in such a hurry to get back here and see you, you old coot."

Now Joe's smile had stretched to a full one.

"Why don't you get back in there and give her another hug?" Ryan asked.

There was a soft noise behind them, and they turned in tandem. Ashley stood just inside the doorway, alone, and had obviously heard at least part of their conversation. Her eyes were soft and even a little shimmery.

She sniffled, and then Joe moved toward her. They met in the middle in a full-on embrace.

Over his shoulder, her eyes met Ryan's. And held.

He didn't smile. He knew this had to be tough on her. It had to have been hard enough to come home without her arm, but to find her parents' in such precarious health...he couldn't imagine.

He nodded to her once, a silent promise to do everything he could to make things easier on her.

Ash turned up at the feed store too early the next morning.

She found the employee door unlocked and the lights in the back storage room on. And the office.

She would always think of the ten by ten room as her dad's office, but when she turned the corner, it was Ryan spread across the black computer chair, his long legs kicked to the side, chewing on a Bic pen.

He looked up, probably alerted by the clicking of Atlas's toenails on the floor.

"We were out for our morning run," she said. She smoothed back her hair, wet with sweat and still rumpled from sleep. She straightened her running shorts and T-shirt and wished suddenly she'd had a shower before coming here.

He smiled so wide, she wondered if it made his cheeks ache. "I'm glad you came in. Just a sec."

He leaned forward, hands going to the keyboard. She looked over his shoulder to see what looked like some kind of time-keeping program. He blanked the screen and then turned back to her, sweeping a coffee mug off the desk and offering it to her.

"No thanks." Drinking his coffee would have been too intimate.

She was still a little shaken after yesterday. That kiss. And then seeing his gentle way with her dad. He'd comforted her dad when she hadn't even registered anything had been wrong. Oh, it had been noisy at the party, busy with all the people and activity. She could excuse herself for that.

But the truth was, Ryan knew her parents better now than she did.

And seeing his patient way with her father had touched a chord inside her. Made her realize that maybe there was more to the man than the prankster he used to be.

"I was thinking," he started, "do you want to go out this weekend? I could make a reservation..."

His voice trailed off as she shook her head. "No, thanks."

Everything was so muddled right now, with her parents' health and trying to find a new job or direction. She couldn't add dating Ryan into the mix. Right?

He accepted with grace, his smile unwavering. "Okay."

She needed a distraction. But glancing around the office didn't provide one. The two goldenrod metal filing cabinets in the corner were the same, but the desk had been updated to a newer model. How had he gotten that by her old-fashioned father? They probably needed it to accommodate the computer.

"I'm used to seeing it messier," she murmured.

He chuckled. "Joe accused me of throwing away his important paperwork the first time I cleaned it after he promoted me. I never could understand how he found anything in those piles and piles of papers."

She lowered her gaze and caught on the large desk calendar. Yesterday's date had been circled in red, twice, with her name scrawled in the center.

She felt hot, remembering the impromptu welcoming crowd he'd gathered.

Ryan nudged her off-center, and she didn't like it. She'd come here to see if she could find some answers, maybe start finding her place again.

"Will you show me around this morning? I want to start taking over some of my dad's duties." She didn't like to be idle, and until she figured out what she was going to do now, she wanted to take some of the weight off her dad's shoulders. But like Ryan had told her yesterday, the business had changed since she'd left home at nineteen. She'd need some new training if she wanted to help out.

"Sure," he said easily. "I've got a shipment arriving in a little while, but we've got time." He stood up, and the room seemed suddenly smaller, as if his presence sucked the air right out.

She turned and motioned Atlas into the hall, her hand tense on the leash.

This was crazy.

She couldn't be attracted to Ryan. Annoying Ryan. Two years her junior, during high school he'd followed her around like the president and only member of her fan club.

He'd started it yesterday with that kiss. This attraction was all his fault. Until that moment in the airport, she'd never thought of him this way before.

Sure, they'd had some fun times together working in the store during high school, but he'd just been a kid. An adolescent more interested in football and rodeoing than anything else.

But a decade later...? That boy was tall, broad, and handsome. And as far as she could tell, he was also intelligent, capable, and kind. That boy had turned into some kind of man.

Why did she have to realize that now? Now, when she didn't know who she was any longer. An ex-soldier. An amputee. A veteran with no goals, no plans.

She needed direction.

"We updated the break room last year..."

Ryan ushered her forward, seemingly unaware of her internal turmoil. He propped open the door to the employee-only area, and she saw the same old olive-green fridge that had been there for years, the same Formica table, and a collection of slightly off-kilter chairs. But there was a relatively new flat-panel TV in one corner.

She raised her brows at Ryan, and he winked. "If you're on the Saturday staff, you want to be able to keep an eye on the football games during break time."

She rolled her eyes.

He took her up into the showroom, which she almost

didn't recognize. There were the familiar items, rows of dog and cat food, horse bridles, and saltlicks for cattle.

But there was a display of small pet supplies—items for rabbits, fish, rodents—that she'd never seen before.

And she saw several racks of clothing items, from hats to boots, overalls to coveralls, flannel, cotton, and denim.

"These are new." A length of slack in Atlas's leash, she reached out and touched one of the country-chic denim dresses, prominently placed where someone walking into the store would easily see it.

"They're on consignment from a local lady who designs them."

She'd been so engrossed in the clothing, she hadn't seen Ryan circle the store. He was walking toward them from the right, approaching Atlas's deaf side.

And she didn't realize it until too late.

Atlas turned and the saw the threat of Ryan's tall body in his space. Everything happened too fast.

The dog tensed.

"Wait—" She pulled against the leash. Too much slack. Not enough time.

It was too late. The dog lunged before Ryan even knew what was happening, his powerful jaw clamping over Ryan's hand.

"Atlas, *out*," she issued the command, and even though her voice was shaking, the dog released Ryan.

Blood dripped down his hand and onto the floor.

"Oh, Ryan!"

He clapped his other hand over the bite. "It's okay—"

"I'm so sorry. That's his deaf side—the explosion—" She was stammering, and shaking. "He didn't see you."

Ryan looked up at her with those steady eyes.

"Ashley. It's okay. I'm okay."

"Y-you're bleeding." A little rivulet of blood trailed through his clasped fingers and dripped on the floor.

She closed her eyes as disjointed images filled her mind—her own body, covered in gore. Atlas bloodied from the IED.

She tensed, gasped, searched the darkness for something to hang onto, something to pull her back to the present.

"Ashley. Ash."

Something bumped her, and her eyes flew open. Ryan was there, close. His hands were still clamped together, the good one holding the injured one, but his shoulder must've bumped hers, his attempt to pull her back.

He'd seen too much. She knew that by the compassion shining in his eyes.

But he didn't ask if she was okay. She wasn't.

"Are you all right?" Her throat was scratchy, and she cleared it, attempting to rid it of emotion.

"Yeah. He barely got me. I'll clean it out in the bathroom. You want to come with me and see for yourself?"

Moments later, she found herself stuffed in the tiny employee bathroom with Ryan, the door propped open so she could see Atlas lying in the hall outside. The glare of the fluorescent lights burned her eyes. It had to be the lights, right? She was a soldier, and soldiers didn't get emotional.

He ran cold water over his hand and, as the blood turned pink and drained into the sink, she saw that he'd been right. Atlas's teeth had mostly grazed the soft, fleshy part of his palm beneath his thumb.

"Hand me the first-aid kit," he said, indicating a shelf by the door.

It was heavier than it looked, the weight off balance inside the plastic box, and she bobbled it, almost sending it crashing to the floor before she caught it against her middle. Frustrated with her limitations, she grunted as she smacked it down a little too hard on top of the commode.

She rummaged for gauze while he soaped up the cut, hissing a little through his teeth.

"Are you sure you don't need stitches?"

"See for yourself." He lifted his hand, and she set the gauze on top of the open kit and grabbed his wrist. His skin was cool beneath hers.

The blood flow had slowed considerably. Really, it was

more of a scrape than a puncture.

"Help me wrap it?"

She did, their fingers tangling once, sending a hot flash up her spine and the back of her neck. The fumble made her reach for words. "Atlas is deaf on his right side—the side where his ear is scarred. If he doesn't see you coming—"

"I didn't realize," he said. She held the end of the gauze as he stuck a piece of white tape across it, but before she could pull away, he'd turned his hand over and clasped her fingers.

"If you want to talk about...anything, I'm here."

Before she could rip her hand away, he let her go and moved past her to crouch in the doorway. Far enough that he'd have a half-second of warning, but Atlas only looked at him, mouth open and panting.

"Sorry, old boy," Ryan said. "Didn't mean to scare you." He didn't reach out, an action that someone else might've done. Instead, he let the dog associate his scent, remember who he was from the truck ride.

In the whole thing, Ryan hadn't lost his calm.

"Did you lose hearing in your ear as well?" he asked without turning back to her.

It was easier answering him when he wasn't looking at her. He was probably smart enough to figure that out on his own. "Part." She made a *click* with her tongue and teeth and Atlas rose to his feet, then licked Ryan's chin.

After enduring it for a moment, he said, "All right," with a little laugh.

When he stood up in the small space, he was too close.

Her memories took her momentarily back at the airport terminal when he'd kissed her. He looked down on her, eyes serious but somehow still smiling.

"I'll remember." Whether he was talking about Atlas or her, she didn't know. But somehow, she knew this was a promise he would keep.

CHAPTER THREE

Later that week, Ashley tapped her pencil on the list she'd just written.

She hated looking at her handwriting. Writing with her left hand was torturous. It took forever and her words scrawled across the page, uneven letters making her efforts look like they'd been written by a kindergartener.

But she needed the list. She'd been at the feed store every day, getting the feel of the place and meeting the staff of five. Ryan had given her a copy of the last year's financial records and inventories, and she was attempting to figure them out. Back in high school, she'd only been responsible for the register and stocking shelves, not any of the financial stuff.

Her head was swimming with numbers.

She propped her elbow on the desk in her father's home office, then put her chin on her fist and stared out the back window. The familiar yard hadn't changed much since she'd been in high school. Her mom's flower beds were well-maintained. She wondered if her mom had gotten someone to help since her attack. Either way, she was here now, and she could help.

Everything was so different at home. Her mother was noticeably weaker, slower. Her father's Alzheimer's made him lucid some days and difficult to deal with on others.

And Ashley had missed it all.

Guilt panged, a familiar companion since she'd been home. She'd missed so much time with her parents, all because of her selfishness. She'd been hurt, so she'd punished them by staying away, by making a new life for herself. But it didn't change that they were the ones who had cared for her, had raised her.

Was she too late to make up for all she'd lost? She saw how the worry ate at her mom. Had that contributed to the heart attack?

Ashley needed to find the right time and apologize, to ask for forgiveness. She couldn't change the past, but she was here now, and she was ready to reclaim a relationship with her parents.

And while she'd been off on the other side of the world, apparently Ryan had been here for her parents. He must've been, because he appeared everywhere she looked these days.

She'd gone into the store at different times, and he always seemed to be there. Except of course when he'd driven her father to a doctor's appointment in the city two days ago. She'd wanted to do it herself, but one of the big things on her rehab list was arranging for and learning to drive a modified car, one that could be operated with only one arm.

He'd been around so much, most of the time she wasn't sure if she was coming or going.

And he always seemed too happy to see her. And lately, he'd usually had a treat for Atlas.

But what had happened to his dreams of owning land and raising horses? It was all he'd talked about back in high school. It had been over a decade ago, but she still remembered it. Surely he hadn't given up on his dreams for all the big bucks he was making at the feed store.

Movement behind her, and she turned in the desk chair to see her dad walk in the door. His face softened when he saw her. She hadn't seen him since that morning, but by the look in his eyes, he must remember her.

"Ashley-girl, what are you doing in here? Messing with my business things?"

There hadn't appeared to be business *things*, at least not dated in the last year or so, in the office at all until she'd brought the financial records and inventories Ryan had given her. But she smiled anyway. "I haven't touched anything. Just thinking about... what I'm supposed to be doing now."

He came closer, and she stood to meet him in the middle of the room.

"What can I do for the store?" she asked. "I'd love to take some of the duties off Ryan's hands—"

"Ryan? He's a good boy. He took on extra hours this summer when one of the other girls quit."

She paused, unsure. From the way the other employees talked, Ryan had been acting manager for years, even before her dad had officially named him that. But her father might be caught in the past.

"I could take over the bookkeeping from Ryan, or at least start there and see what other duties I could take over."

"Why would you want to do that? I thought you're leaving for boot camp next week?"

Ashley half-turned to put her missing arm further out of his line of sight. Sometimes, when he was caught in the past, seeing her as she was now disturbed him.

"I'm staying here," she said gently. She didn't bother telling him the rest. She'd probably told him a dozen times this week already.

It was obvious she wasn't going to get any lucid answers out of him this evening. "Do you smell that?" she said, sniffing the air. "Smells like dinner's almost ready." She turned him toward the kitchen and inched along with him.

In the kitchen, a male voice joined her mother's, and Ashley drew up short in the doorway. Her father crossed the kitchen to sit across the nook table from her mother.

Ryan was chopping something on the cutting board and had two pots going on the stovetop.

"Hey," he greeted her over his shoulder.

"What are you doing here?"

"Making supper," came his easy reply.

"Ryan took a cooking class a couple months ago and needed someone to try out his recipes on," her mother explained. She seemed to be doing absolutely nothing—other than sitting and visiting with Ryan. Good for her.

"Wanna help?" he asked cheerfully.

"I guess." She moved closer to him and registered the quantity of food spread out on the counter. "We'll never eat all this."

"Ryan usually leaves us with the leftovers. He eats at the local café too much," her mother chided.

Ryan didn't stop chopping but grinned, and Ashley suddenly knew what was happening. He'd found another way to care for her parents. If he cooked for her parents twice a week and left them with leftovers enough for two meals, her mom would have to spend much less time in the kitchen. Helping again.

He glanced up and saw when she got it. He winked. Totally unruffled.

"What do you want me to do?" she asked through the unwelcome emotion clogging her throat.

He was making some kind of pasta dish. "We'll need to get the noodles in water once it starts boiling, and open that jar of sauce."

She'd seen the large jar of red sauce and was way ahead of him. She opened the drawer and pulled out two of the grippy pads her physical therapist had suggested, setting one on the counter and putting the jar on top of it. She took the other pad and gripped the lid of the jar with it.

"Ashley, let me do that for you." Ryan was suddenly at her elbow, his vegetables abandoned on the chopping block.

"I can do it," she said firmly without taking her gaze from her task. She was still learning ways of coping with her disability, but this was something she could do. Even if it took more than one try to get the right angle, the right grip, she would muscle open the jar.

"Aw, c'mon. It'll make me feel like a manly-man. Let me do it for you." She knew he was teasing, but it didn't change anything.

"If you do it *for* me," she said quietly, "I'll feel like less of a person."

He went still beside her.

113

She half-expected him to argue or get offended, but he returned to his chopping board without a fuss.

Same old laid back Ryan.

It was she who was on edge.

Ryan finished chopping the mushrooms and moved on to the red pepper, trying not to show how Ashley's quiet revelation had pummeled him like a punch in the gut.

He would never want to make her feel less than she was. So he'd stood back and let her struggle to get that jar open, even though he could've done it in a couple seconds.

She'd always been independent. It was probably a good thing that she *wanted* to do the same tasks she'd done before. He'd even overheard her talking with her mom about getting a modified car so she could drive herself around.

It irritated him, just a little bit, because he wanted her to have a reason to keep him around. He wouldn't mind if she leaned on him. He was using every opportunity to get her in the store to show how they could work together.

"Mrs. Patterson stopped in today. Her mare's about to foal again," he told Joe as he chopped the onion. He'd put it off until last, because he hated slicing onions.

"The big black?" Joe asked.

That horse had been gone for several years. Joe must have been having a bad day. So Ryan didn't correct him about the horse. Instead, he said, "A chestnut. Mrs. P. is hoping for a stallion, wants to have a new bloodline in the next couple years."

At Ryan's side, Ashley pointed to the pot that had come to a rolling boil, and he nodded to the box of pasta. She reached for the box and upended it into the water, splashing hot water over the side because she didn't have a second hand to catch it before it hit the water's surface. The droplets sizzled on the stovetop.

She frowned. "What about you?" she asked. "I remember you wanted to have a nice-sized spread and raise horses."

That was one of his biggest dreams, second only to his

desire to have Ashley fall in love with him. Of course, she didn't know about that one. That she cared enough to remember about his horses spread warmth through his chest.

"I'm boarding a couple horses at my cousin's place. I'm still gonna get some land when the time is right." He wasn't *that* old yet. He'd had more important things to work on while she'd been overseas fighting for their country.

"Wouldn't you make more headway if you got a different job, maybe went back to school?"

Right. She thought he was a college dropout and a flake. She was a smart cookie, and he trusted that she would figure out why he'd made the choices he had. He could be patient.

But deep down, it bothered him that she thought so little of him. He pushed it aside.

"It'll happen when it's supposed to happen." He looked over his shoulder to Joe. "Bluebell is having puppies again."

The old man chuckled. "So the Russells are in a fight again?"

"Yep," Ryan answered.

Ashley looked at him sideways, so he explained. "Bert Russell's been breeding prize-winning Irish Setter puppies for the last several years. Every litter, his wife threatens to leave him, because she doesn't want to clean up after their messes and deal with crying puppies keeping her up all night."

"But she never does," Joe called out. "What's this, the third or fourth litter?"

"Seventh," Ryan said under his breath. No need to upset Joe about his memory problems and ruin a friendly conversation. "She's threatening more than leaving him this time," Ryan said loud enough that Joe would hear. "She wants to go to marriage counseling. The way they bicker in the store, I almost thought about telling her we could charge her for forcing us to listen."

"But you didn't dare," Joe guessed, and they shared a chuckle.

Ryan missed having Joe around the store. He'd taken on more of the duties so Joe wouldn't have to worry about keeping track of the financials or missing out on ordering or paying vendors, but Joe had always been a friend first, especially since Ryan didn't have a dad to look up to.

Ryan finished chopping the onion, put the knife down, sniffed a couple of times, and wiped his drippy nose with his sleeve.

Ashley was watching him so he winked at her. "I'm a sensitive guy."

She rolled her eyes, but there was a hint of a smile playing around her lips.

He did a cursory wash of his hands and then dried off with a dishtowel.

"All right," he said. "You cooking or watching?"

"Cooking, I guess."

He nodded her to the stove, where he'd heated a large skillet. "Let's put some olive oil in, get it nice and hot for our veggies."

She followed his directions and drizzled some oil in, then allowed him to scrape the veggies from his cutting board into the pan.

He pointed her to the pieces of sausage he'd sliced earlier and set aside. "Those are next."

"Did you really take a cooking class?" she asked, looking at him curiously. She tossed the sausages in one at a time.

"Yep. Figured if I was gonna be a bachelor awhile longer, I might as well figure out how to make some things—so I only have to rely on the cafe some of the time, right Mary?"

Ashley's mother agreed and then bent her head to say something privately to Joe.

"Plus, I figured it might be a skill that would help me win you over," Ryan said to Ashley, straight-faced.

She looked panicked for a moment, then stumped, like she didn't know whether he was serious or not.

He winked at her again and nodded to the pan, "Don't burn those onions. We want a nice caramelization on them."

She gave the onions a stir with a long wooden spoon, then turned and pointed the spoon at his chest.

"Don't think I don't know what you're doing."

"What's that?" He kinda liked it when she got sassy with him.

"You might've charmed my parents and my dog, but I'm immune."

She looked so serious that he had to smile. She waved the spoon around like a weapon, so he put his hands up in front of him like he was in the middle of a stick-up.

"You sure about that? I saw you checking me out in the store yesterday."

"I was *not*," she protested.

But the beautiful color flooding her cheeks said otherwise.

She wasn't immune to him. He just needed a little more time to win her over.

He hoped.

CHAPTER FOUR

Ashley stood on the second-story landing outside Ryan's apartment. There was only one small apartment complex in town, as most people lived in the small bungalows that had mostly been built in the fifties, or out on their farms.

She had a hard time imagining him living here. Ryan was larger than life. He'd talked about horses and land so much in high school. And she knew his mom had moved out of town shortly after he'd graduated.

Why would he choose to stay here when he could've found a higher-paying job in Oklahoma City? The job with her parents was a dead-end. Even with a small annual raise every year, it would take him years to save enough to buy land. And horses weren't cheap to care for.

He was fun, personable, and the customers at the store loved him. She'd always considered him a friend.

But he was going nowhere.

And she had to find a path for herself.

So why was she here? After a supper of laughter and stories—mostly from their teen years when they'd worked together—he'd taken his leave but had forgotten the notebook she'd seen him carrying around the store. She'd flipped through it out of idle curiosity. Notes, to-do lists, ideas for seasonal promotions, even a grocery list. Some people might carry a smart phone, but apparently, Ryan kept all his data the old-fashioned way.

No wonder he'd written her all those letters.

So she'd used the notebook as an excuse. She brought it to

his apartment, knowing he'd need it, and hoping for the opportunity to tell him what she needed to say. She had to tell him to stop pursuing her. She wasn't interested.

No matter how charming he was, or that he could cook, or that he had a certain way with her father, keeping him calm and telling him stories and making him feel like he was still involved at the store. That stuff wouldn't win her over.

She wasn't interested.

She forced herself to knock on the door.

He opened it with his phone to his ear. His entire face creased with a smile when he caught sight of her, and her stomach swooped low. He motioned her in.

"Just a sec, okay?" he whispered as she passed him.

She and Atlas slipped through the doorway behind him. She settled the dog on the floor near the door and brought the book with her into the small living room, clutching it like a shield against her midsection.

Ryan's apartment was masculine and neat. A somewhat-battered couch took up most of the living area and was opposite a large flat-screen TV. He had books strewn across the coffee table, several open and more notebooks open with pens lying across them. What was this?

He'd paced into the kitchen but she could clearly hear his side of the conversation.

"I can deliver an order that size, no problem. Sweet feed. And corn. Just like last time."

She sat down on the couch, tapping his store notebook against her knee.

"It'll have to be Friday night, 'cause I've got a class tomorrow evening."

What class was he talking about? Another cooking class?

Her eyes fell to the nearest book. *Strategic Management.*

It was a college textbook. It looked like advanced-level coursework. The lined notebook next to it was open and full of hastily-scribbled notes in Ryan's handwriting.

"All right. Yes. Thanks, Mr. S. I'll see you Friday. G'bye."

He re-appeared in the archway between the kitchen alcove

and the living area, squatted down with one of his homemade treats, and patted his knee.

Atlas looked to her first, and she clicked her tongue to let the dog know it was okay. He padded over to Ryan and took the treat, licking Ryan's hand for good measure.

"Doing business after hours?" she asked.

"Sometimes."

"How often?" She already knew he put in more hours at the store than anyone else.

"Some folks don't have a truck or don't like to get out. Doesn't cost me much to deliver their orders, and the store gets their business. And sometimes a referral."

She shook her head. He was a good guy.

But that didn't mean she could date him. She had enough going on with her parents.

"I noticed the sales numbers for this month seem a little flat," she said. She hadn't meant to come here to talk business, but what she had come to say was going to be so uncomfortable.

"We'll have a spike this weekend." He stood and stepped into the living room. "You want a soda or something?"

She shook her head and held out the notebook. "You forgot this."

"Oh. Thanks."

Her eyes fell on the coffee table again, and then she looked back at him. "Are you... you're taking college classes?"

"Yep."

She couldn't help but ask, "Since when?"

"Since my freshman year." He seemed to know she was floundering. "I was able to go full time those first two years, then things changed"—he shrugged as if it hadn't mattered all that much—"and I started taking night classes. Takes a little longer that way, but that's okay."

"So you never dropped out."

He shook his head.

But he'd let her think that at the airport, hadn't he? Or had he just handled her the way he handled her dad? He'd known she was wary and upset her first day back, tired from traveling and shaken from the other things he'd told her about her parents.

Had he just been protecting her feelings?

He crossed his powerful arms over his chest. "There's probably a lot about me you don't know. I'm not fourteen anymore."

She shook her head. Didn't know what to say. "I'm still two years older than you." Stupid thing to say. How was that helpful?

"Maybe if you read my letters, you'd find out what kind of man I am."

She stood up. "I have to go."

He followed her to the door. "You wanna go out this weekend?"

"No."

But after she and Atlas had escaped into the parking lot, she didn't know why she hadn't told him to quit asking. That's what she'd gone in there intending to say.

But Ryan had spent years working on his education. He hadn't dropped out like she'd thought. That made her see him a differently.

Everything he did surprised her.

Maybe he was right. Maybe she should read those letters of his. What else would they reveal about him?

But did she really want to know?

She didn't know what she was supposed to be doing with herself. She didn't have time for a relationship. She didn't have the head space.

Did she?

Ashley decided she was going to stay away from Ryan all weekend. She needed some breathing room to get her head on straight.

She needed to figure out what was going on with the feed store so she could find out if she was needed there or if she should be seeking work somewhere else.

But when she and Atlas took their late-morning jog, she was shocked to see a line of people and animals outside the store. Several people greeted her as she passed the throng and went into the back of the store.

She found Ryan in the office, hunched forward in the desk chair and squinting at the computer screen, a pen clamped between his teeth.

"What's going on?" she asked.

He started and looked up at her guiltily. With one click, whatever had been on the screen disappeared, replaced by the store's logo. "Good morning, sunshine. Rethinking going on that date with me?"

"No," she said firmly. "What are you doing?"

He retained the vaguely guilty look. "Reports."

She raised her eyebrows, but he didn't say more. Was something going on? She had a stray thought that perhaps she should check the paperwork he'd given her. Would she even know what to look for if Ryan wasn't being up front about the books? How long had it been since her father had really known what was going on in the store?

But that thought almost seemed silly. Ryan would never do something like cheat her parents. Would he?

"What are all those people and animals doing outside?"

"Vet weekend."

His words made no sense to her. "Excuse me?"

"The veterinarian from the next town over comes down one Saturday a month and gives discounted services for three hours. Gets him some new customers and gets people in the store. I told you sales would pick up this weekend, didn't I?"

It did make sense. In fact, if it hadn't been Ryan, she might've said it was a brilliant idea.

It seemed like another way that Ryan had made himself invaluable to her parents. He kept the store afloat, even in a struggling economy.

He cooked them supper twice a week.

He took them to doctor's appointments.

But those were her jobs, not his.

If she couldn't do those things, what was she supposed to do?

CHAPTER FIVE

Ashley went through the previous month's time sheets again. Matched up the paychecks to the expense ledger. The expense ledger showed the same expense month after month, with very little variation.

But she still suspected something wasn't right. Something funny was going on. Ryan had blanked the computer screen twice now when she'd come into the office. What was he doing that he didn't want her to see?

She'd gone so far back in the paperwork that she'd seen her own handwritten timecards from twelve years ago. She couldn't find anything out-of-the-ordinary.

In fact, she'd given herself a headache looking at all the numbers and flipping through spreadsheet after spreadsheet.

She rubbed the back of her neck and stood up from her father's home office chair. Her mom had gone to visit a friend for the afternoon. Dad had been resting, and she'd started the project when the quiet of the house had started to get to her.

She tiptoed up the stairs to look in on him, but his bedroom was empty, late afternoon sunlight filtering in through the curtains. The bedsheets were rumpled, but he wasn't there.

"Dad?" she asked.

No answer.

She walked down the hall to the bathroom. Peeked in her bedroom, just to be sure.

Back downstairs, through the dining room and kitchen.

"Dad?" Her voice rose, and she started shaking.

Had he been moving around, and she hadn't heard because she'd been that caught up in her project?

She swept back through the house and noticed the front door was cracked. Had it been that way when she'd gone upstairs, and she'd missed it?

That's when she really started to panic. Her palm grew moist, tongue cleaved to the roof of her mouth as her pulse went wild. Her mom had the car. So at least he couldn't drive anywhere.

What should she do?

Her mom had a cell phone but rarely answered it. Ash called anyway. "Come on! Pick up, pick up." When she heard her mother's familiar voice mail message, she hung up. No sense scaring her mom to death.

Should she call the police?

She ran out into the street with bare feet and looked both directions, but she couldn't see her father anywhere.

She tried her mom again. "C'mon, mom. Pick up."

She didn't know her mom's friend's phone number.

Her heart thundered in her ears as she dialed Ryan.

He picked up right away. "Hey, Ashley. What's up?"

"Um..." Tears filled her eyes, temporarily blinding her. Emotion clogged her throat. Her completely irrational reaction proved just how far from the cool-headed soldier she'd become.

"What's wrong?"

She thought she heard keys jingling in the background, like he was ready to rush to her rescue.

It calmed her, a little.

She didn't need help. She could find her dad. She just needed to think straight.

"I'm probably overreacting." She was relieved to find her voice steady. "I think my dad left the house. I can't find him—" A hiccup surprised her and broke off her sentence.

"I'll be there in two minutes."

"You don't have to—" Her rising hysteria overwhelmed her.

"Ashley." His voice was as calm and implacable, as always. "I know."

She hung up and ran inside to put her shoes on.

They found him in a neighbor's backyard, two streets over. Joe was wearing pajama bottoms, a T-shirt, and floppy house slippers.

Ashley ran up to him and hugged him while Ryan watched from the sidewalk.

He could barely believe she'd called him. He didn't kid himself he'd been the first dial, but she'd called him nonetheless.

And he'd been here for her. Surely she would see him differently now.

He heard the tears in her voice as she reprimanded her dad. The old man seemed shaky and tearful as well. He kept glancing at Ashley's injured arm.

But when he saw Ryan, his face relaxed.

"You scared us, Joe," Ryan said, moving forward and clapping the older man on the shoulder.

"I'm...sorry."

Joe was docile as they loaded him into the passenger side of Ryan's truck. Ashley walked around the truck with Ryan, so she could slide into the middle seat.

"Thank you for coming," she said, face to the ground. "Even though you didn't have to."

Maybe she was embarrassed that she'd needed help.

He could still see the tremor in her hand.

It gave him the courage to pull her into his arms. She came willingly, and her arm slipped around his back.

He breathed into the crown of her hair and held her. And she hung on to him. And that gave him hope.

Finally, her tremors slowed.

"Why did you come?" she whispered.

She eased back in his arms, but he'd finally gotten her here, and he wasn't in a hurry to let go. He kept one arm loosely around her waist and raised the other to cup her face gently.

"You know why."

He let his thumb slide across the softness of her cheek. "I love you, Ashley."

Her eyes flicked down, closing him off from the vibrant blue depths. A little crease appeared between her eyebrows, and she shook her head minutely, like she could refute the fact.

She couldn't.

"But I... You haven't even seen me in years," she breathed. "And I don't know what I'm doing. I barely know my own parents any more. And what kind of a person lets that happen? I don't know what I'm going to do next..."

Her words trailed off and she shook her head, half-turning her face into his palm.

"I have always loved you, Ash."

Her eyes opened, gaze flying up to meet his. He read the vulnerability in their depths, the questioning...maybe even the yearning.

He couldn't resist. He dipped his head and kissed her.

It wasn't the time for something big, not with Joe in the truck and Ashley still upset, so he just let it be a sweet brush of his lips against hers, then backed off.

He tucked her into the cab of the truck and slid in beside her.

"Since I did come to your rescue, I figure you owe me." He winked when she tipped her head at him. "Go out with me next weekend. I've got this family thing. Actually, I'm kind of getting an award. You can be my date."

She shook her head slightly. Did that mean *no*? Or what? But now wasn't the time to push her.

When they pulled into Ashley's driveway, her mom was standing on the porch steps, wringing her hands.

He helped Ashley out of the car, and she grabbed his hand, completely stalling his heart.

"Okay."

Then she shocked the life back into him when she leaned up and brushed a kiss across his cheek. "And thank you," she whispered before she rounded the truck to tell her mom what happened.

Later that night, after they'd had a quiet supper and she and her mom had gotten her dad tucked into bed, Ashley sat down across the table from her mom, where both of them nursed cups of hot tea.

"I wish you'd told me how bad Dad had gotten," she said softly.

Her mom wrapped one hand around the teacup, looking down. "We'd already grown so far apart."

Ashley's chest tightened. Tighter than it had been. "I know. I'm sorry, Mom. I was...I was wrong to stay away."

Ashley set her teacup on the table, and her mom reached out. She grabbed Ashley's hand and held on. Tears pricked Ashley's eyes.

"Your dad and I never meant to hurt you. We should've told you sooner that you were adopted. But, as far as we were concerned, you were our daughter." She shrugged a little. "We never thought of you as anything else."

Ashley squeezed her mom's hand. "I just...I forgot."

She took a deep breath, took a moment to push back the threatening tears. "I'm sorry you didn't feel like you could tell me about Dad."

"What would you have done? Given up your career to come home and sit with him? You wouldn't have been happy."

"Sometimes life isn't about being happy. It's about being with the people you love. Who need you."

Saying the words aloud brought her mind to Ryan.

He'd been there for her parents when she couldn't. He hadn't been out chasing his dream of owning land and horses. He'd changed his college plans to study part-time so he could take on more hours, more responsibility for the store.

Thinking about Ryan immediately led her to think about his declaration. She'd managed to keep her mind on other things, skittering around his *I love you*, but now, with the house quiet around them, it came back to her.

Could she really trust in his love?

He wasn't anything like the ornery, fun-loving teenager she remembered. He was still full of laughter and joked around, easy-going and patient.

But he was more than that. She was learning he was a man she could depend on.

Her mother squeezed her hand and brought her back to the moment. "At first, your dad didn't want you to worry. We knew you were in danger overseas, and if you were worrying about him, you might not be thinking enough about yourself. Then..."

Her mom wiped beneath her eyes with her free hand.

Dad's situation was hard on all of them. The mood swings, the way he didn't always know who they were. Most distressing was his reaction to her arm. Since he couldn't remember it had happened, every time he saw it from his Alzheimer's-muddled mind, he grieved all over again. She hated the way seeing her gave him such pain.

And it must've been ten times worse on her mom.

"And then your heart attack. I can't believe you didn't tell me when you came to Maryland."

Her mom clasped Ashley's hand, squeezing hard. "I wanted you to get better. You were so weak, so out of it. It hurt to see you like that."

"It hurt to find out from someone else that I'd missed something that scary in my mother's life."

The tears pooled in Ashley's eyes. She gently removed her hand from her mother's and wiped them away with her fingertips. She wasn't one to cry, but the whole situation with her parents was a minefield of emotions.

"So what do we do now?" Ashley asked. "I can take over whatever needs to be done with the feed store—"

"Ryan manages things well," her mom said. "There's not much to do."

"Unless I took over the manager job, like dad always did."

"And put Ryan out of a job? He's been a big help to us—"

"I know." Ashley rubbed her forehead. "But his position also eats into our profits. And if dad eventually needs to go to a care center, that's going to be expensive."

"We've got a lease on the farmland," Mom said. "That brings in some revenue every harvest."

"I thought the farm had been sold. Didn't you say Dad was thinking about selling?" Her parents had owned a couple hundred acres outside of town. When they'd been Ashley's age, they'd run crops and kept animals, but the feed store had become their main income, and the farm had become nothing more than her dad's unrealized childhood dream. She remembered a tinny long-distance phone call about selling the land, but that had been maybe three years ago...

"We stopped being able to plant and harvest, but your father wasn't ready to sell. The lease brings in money."

"But wouldn't it bring a whole lot more if we sold it?"

"Your father would never want to do that."

"He wouldn't want things to be hard on you either, even if he can't tell you that."

Her mother's eyes were washed in tears, and Ashley figured maybe it was time to stop talking about hard things. For now. It had been an emotional day for them all.

She got up and gave her mom a hug. "I'm here now. We're going to work through things together."

It wasn't direction, like Ashley had been hoping for. Waiting on her father patiently was probably going to be harder than anything she'd done on the front lines.

Inaction wasn't easy for her.

But her father had supported her military career and never asked for anything. Ashley owed this to him. After the way she'd treated her parents when she found out she'd been adopted, she owed them both.

If Ryan could be there for her father, she could, too.

She didn't know what to do about the handsome cowboy-slash-manager. She'd agreed to a date—in a moment of weakness—but with everything going on in her family, she wasn't sure she could open her heart.

Was she wrong to take the risk?

CHAPTER SIX

Ryan's big date turned out to be his college graduation. The small regional campus was a forty-five drive from Redbud Trails. How had Ryan kept up with his education, working full-time?

She was a little offended that he hadn't told her he was about to graduate when she'd found the textbooks in his apartment.

"Ryan ain't one to brag about himself," his cousin Maddox told her from two seats down in the noisy auditorium. "But we're real proud of him."

Ryan had disappeared to dress for the graduation ceremony, leaving her with his family. Trusting that she would fit in.

She'd been absorbed by his somewhat-noisy family. Maddox was a quiet, serious cowboy, while Justin, Maddox's brother, teased almost as must as Ryan did. He used a crutch to get around, and he didn't have a cast or anything indicating a recent injury. She hadn't been brave enough to ask what had happened.

Ryan's mother hadn't been able to come from out-of-state, but Justin fiddled with a video camera, determined to tape the ceremony for her.

Maddox's girlfriend Haley and niece Livy, a little girl that Maddox had custody of, had provided some buffer from the two cowboys who seemed determined to tease their cousin mercilessly. Ryan took it all with good grace—which was not a big surprise.

The ceremony started with an invocation and two long speeches. Finally, the procession began. She saw Ryan's blond curls where he stood in line along one wall of the gym.

"You don't think he'd do something ornery, do you?" she asked Haley in a whisper. Like toss a football into the crowd or other hijinks she'd heard of ornery grads doing?

"Ryan?" Haley asked, surprised by the question. "I doubt it. He's pretty responsible. He helped out Maddox a lot right after Justin's accident last year."

Of course he had.

Ryan made his way across the stage with no pomp, only a smile and wave when Justin wolf-whistled at him. The crowd chuckled.

When they'd been dismissed and he made his way through the crowd, his gaze kept colliding with hers. Each time it sent a rush of sweet emotion through her.

He joined the circle of their family and accepted handshakes and slaps on the back from his cousins.

She met him with a hug and a whispered, "Congratulations." Her good wishes felt like so little, too little.

She couldn't believe he'd accomplished this on top of everything else. He'd said before that there was plenty of time for his dreams, for his land and horses.

But she would never be as patient as he was. Hadn't she been out chasing her dreams, finding herself when she'd lost everything?

He was almost too good to be true.

After they left the auditorium, the whole group went out for a celebratory meal to a chain American-style restaurant. She found herself squished between him and the girl, Livy.

"Do you like ice cream?" the little girl asked.

"Oh yes," Ashley replied.

"She's a chocolate girl," Ryan confirmed, sliding his arm casually around the back of the curved booth to rest around Ashley's shoulders. She went hot, but didn't shake off his overture.

"Are we going to order some?" Ashley asked.

Livy looked offended, and Ryan laughed.

Maddox and Haley peered over from where they'd been talking to Justin.

"Livy owns a gourmet ice cream business," Ryan explained.

"Oh. How old are you?" Ashley asked.

Livy's chest puffed out with pride. "Twelve. Haley is my business partner."

"I'm practically a silent partner," Haley clarified. "Livy is the brain behind the business."

"I'm an official taste-tester," Ryan added. "It's an unpaid job, but I'm willing to sacrifice for the good of the company."

Livy giggled.

"The perks mostly outweigh the disadvantages. There was one flavor...pistachio something..." Ryan made a funny face, indicating his displeasure.

"As I remember, you have an iron stomach," Ashley said.

"It wasn't my stomach that objected. My tastebuds were still complaining the next day."

"Maybe you should've brushed your teeth, Mr. College Grad," Justin offered. "Now you've got a fancy degree, you're gonna have to use those brains it's taken so long to buy."

Ryan took the good-natured ribbing in stride. "It'll be your turn next, cuz."

"What's your job?" Livy asked, turning to Ashley.

Ryan quieted beside her.

"I used to be in the military."

Livy's eyes got wide. "Like a soldier?"

"Mm-hmm. I worked with a partner, my dog, Atlas. He sniffed out bombs and other things the bad guys didn't want us to find."

"So did you train him yourself?" asked Haley. "I might need to get some tips. Maddox has a huge beast of a dog that could use a little obedience training."

"Emmie wouldn't hurt a fly," Maddox said mildly.

Ryan said, "Ashley broke up a fight between this huge Rotty and a Golden Retriever the other day when the vet was down at the feed store." He turned to her. "Dog training might be right up your alley."

She raised both brows at him. "With one arm?" she asked in a low voice.

He shrugged. "Doesn't affect you with Atlas."

"He's already trained."

His eyes creased as he smiled and changed the subject.

But his comment stuck in her mind.

After dinner, when Maddox's family and Justin took their leave, Ashley and Ryan were left in the curve of the big booth together. The noise of the restaurant had faded some as the evening passed, and families made way for couples dining together.

She turned toward him and bent her knee on the seat between them and rested her arm on the top of the booth.

He was still as close as he had been when the curved booth had been filled with people. He moved his hand to cup her knee and gently squeezed.

"Thanks for coming out with me today."

"You should've told me. I would've brought a card or a gift or something."

"I don't need a gift," he squeezed her knee once more. "You being here was all the gift I wanted."

Warmth slid into her cheeks. "I'm a little surprised Mom and Dad didn't know."

He shrugged. "I didn't want to make a big deal of it."

"It *is* a big deal."

His humility was just another thing to like about him.

A young man in a pair of Wranglers and a plaid shirt with silver snaps—a cowboy shirt—approached the table. "Hey, buddy. What's up?"

Ryan introduced Ashley to his friend, a guy about his age named Luke. They slid out of the booth, ready to go, and Luke followed them to the door. Ryan held the door for her, then clasped her wrist after she stepped into the warm night air. His palm slid against hers, and he intertwined their fingers. He was still talking to his friend, but she had a hard time following the conversation, too focused on the feel of his warm hand enveloping hers.

Yes, she liked Ryan. More and more the longer she was around him.

But holding hands like this? Anyone could see them. Okay, so it was practically dark and the parking lot was nearly deserted. Still...

She was lost in the terrifying joy of holding hands with Ryan when Luke's words broke into her thoughts. "...harvesting the farm next Saturday."

Hadn't her mom had told her the person leasing their farm was going to harvest on that day?

She started shivering.

Surely not. Surely, if Ryan were leasing her parents' land, he would have told her about it.

Ryan cast her a cursory glance, then turned back to Luke, not noticing that anything was wrong. "That's the plan."

Ryan was the lease holder? Why wouldn't he have told her about that? Seemed every time she turned around, she was learning something about him—something he'd hidden from her. He hadn't exactly been secretive about his college classes or graduation, but he hadn't been forthcoming either.

But his life was so intertwined with her parents. The business, the meals, the rides. If everything were on the up and up, why all the secrecy?

And then she remembered how he'd blanked the computer screen when she'd surprised him at the office, as if he hadn't wanted her to see what he'd been doing.

No, Ryan wouldn't do anything unethical. But she couldn't stop her mind from whirling, speeding ahead. Hadn't she been concerned enough to track his hours at the feed store this week by hand?

He laughed at something Luke said. "Sounds good. See you later, man." They watched as the man crossed the parking lot, climbed into his car, and drove away. When he looked back at her, his expression registered concern.

"What's up?" he asked.

"You're harvesting next Saturday afternoon?"

He nodded, expression shuttered.

"My parents' place is being harvested next Saturday."

"Yeah." This time he barely breathed the word.

"You're harvesting my parents' place," she concluded. "You're the lessee."

He nodded again. "Yeah. I was going to tell you."

"When?" she breathed. She ripped her hand away from him.

"I don't know." He turned in profile to her and ran one hand through his hair. "When the timing was better, I guess. I didn't want you to think—"

"Are you—" She couldn't get the words out the first time and had to clear her throat. "Are you taking advantage of my parents?"

He'd started to turn back to her when she spoke, but he froze at her words. All the expression faded from his face.

"Is that really what you think about me? After everything?"

His voice was even, but she'd have to be deaf not to hear the undertone of hurt.

But she was confused, and afraid, too.

"I know you've been falsifying your timecards." She didn't actually have proof. This was the first week she'd kept track of his daily hours, and the week wouldn't roll over until tomorrow.

He held her gaze until she looked away. The back of her eyes were hot, like she was on the verge of tears. But that couldn't be right, either. She didn't care that much, did she?

She cleared her throat again. "Why didn't you tell me about the lease, if it was on the up-and-up?"

He turned away, his shoulders stiff. "I told you everything. In the letters."

"That doesn't count." Her voice was tight. "You should've told me everything that first day when we were driving home from the airport. But instead, you held it back." Then a horrible idea occurred to her, and it almost made her knees buckle. "Okay, so if the contract is fair to my parents, were you...were you keeping it from me like some kind of *ace in the hole* or something? If you couldn't win me any other way, you'd tell me about the lease and guilt me into liking you?"

Not that he'd needed to. She'd liked him just fine.

He stuffed his hat on his head. Didn't turn to her or make a joke. When he spoke, his voice was quiet, resigned. "Honey, if you really think I'm the kind of person who would cheat Joe and Mary, then I guess I didn't have a chance from the start."

Silently, he led the way through the gravel lot to his truck. He held the door for her but kept his head down so his Stetson hid his eyes.

He drove her home, his expression neutral and his eyes on the road. It was the quietest ride she'd ever spent with him.

Maybe she'd hurt him with her accusations, but didn't she deserve the truth?

When he pulled into her parents' drive, she pushed open the door before he'd had a chance to shift into park. "I'm going to call Mom's lawyer tomorrow," she said quietly, then jumped out before he could respond.

Her face burned, and she still felt on the edge of tears as she jogged up the steps to the porch. She expected to hear his tires crunch along the road, but instead, he killed his ignition. She heard his door open just as she reached for the knob.

"Ashley!" His voice was hoarse, full of emotion.

She couldn't face him. Not now.

"Ash." His voice had gone to a lower register, like he could barely get the syllable out.

She turned back at the nickname he so rarely used. He stood with one leg still in the truck, one elbow propped over the open door. His hat cast a shadow over his face, so she couldn't see his eyes.

Would he confess to taking advantage of her parents? To the timecard scheme—or to...whatever it was he was hiding?

"I'll save you the trouble," he said into the darkness. "Your mom keeps all her legal documents in the bottom desk drawer. The locked one. The key is in a little bowl on top of the bookshelf."

Of course he knew that. Because her mom *trusted* him. But

Ashley didn't. Couldn't.

She couldn't speak past the lump in her throat. She rushed inside and slammed the door behind her, then leaned against the inside of the door for long minutes until his truck started up and the sound of its engine faded away.

No one was awake, but her mom had left the kitchen light on. Ash flipped on the office light, squinting in the brightness after the dim truck and interior of the house. The key was right where Ryan had said it would be, but it stuck in the drawer. Angry, so full of emotions, she twisted it violently with her left hand. Then jimmied it. Finally, the lock disengaged and the drawer opened. She flipped through the documents, agonizingly slowly as she maneuvered her fingers to see between the pages.

Bills. Bank statements. A last will and testament and a power of attorney over her father were there, and she blinked back hot moisture that was blurring her vision. She couldn't think about her dad right now. Right behind those, she found the lease in a plain, unmarked manila folder.

The terms didn't make sense. She pulled the drawer open with too much force and pencils and blank white paper spilled across the floor.

She scrubbed at the moisture scalding her cheeks. When she'd settled with her back against the wall with a blank sheet of notebook paper and a pencil, she laboriously wrote the terms out in two columns. And then she'd stared at her little-kid handwriting, confused, even though the truth was right there, in front of her eyes.

She'd been right—partially. It wasn't a fair contract. One party benefited more than the other.

The lease wasn't in Ryan's favor. It was in her parents'.

He *lost* money most seasons. In a good year, he might break even.

Her nose stung and her heart thudded. A snuffle from the door alerted her she wasn't alone as Atlas padded in.

She slung her arm over his neck, taking comfort in his familiar presence. She knew what she wanted to do. Because she had to know.

And she was still dressed.

She slipped Atlas's leash on and took him for a walk. In the dark. The whole three-quarters of a mile to the feed store. Inside, she flipped on the lights in the back and turned off the emergency alarm. Then she headed straight to the office.

It only took a few minutes to boot the computer and pull up the time-entry program. She glanced at the post-it note she'd used to jot down the actual hours Ryan had spent at the feed store working. Her total was 61.25. And it didn't take a genius to see that yes, he'd *fixed* his timecard. He'd taken off hours to show that he'd worked exactly forty. She knew from talking with her mom that Ryan got paid by the hour, not a flat salary. Her father had put the arrangement in place because he didn't want to take advantage of Ryan.

But Ryan was taking advantage of *himself.*

She scrolled back weeks, then months. Ryan's timecard showed forty hours on the dot each week, when all the other employees' showed variations.

She sat back in the office chair and rested her hand on Atlas's head.

He wasn't cheating her parents.

He was cheating himself.

Why?

CHAPTER SEVEN

Two hours later, Ashley was no closer to sleep.

Even in the dark, her eyes strayed to the drawer where she'd stowed Ryan's stack of letters.

He'd done as he'd promised all those years ago. He'd sent her one a week for the entire time she'd been on active duty.

And she'd never read a one of them.

She'd handled them some. Sometimes, when she'd been particularly homesick, she'd take one out of her belongings and look at his masculine scrawl on the address lines. Sometimes, she'd even touched the writing.

But she'd never opened one of them.

What had she been afraid of? That was easy. She'd been afraid of missing home too much. She'd been afraid that reading his words would make her second-guess her career choice and wish she'd stayed in Redbud Trails.

And maybe they would have, or maybe not.

Had she been afraid that she'd fall for him if she read his letters?

Maybe. She'd reluctantly liked him back in high school, but she'd put him off because of the age difference between them.

But while she was in the service, he grew up. They both had.

And she'd fallen for him, anyway, now that she was home.

She ripped the first envelope, trying to get the letter out with only one hand to work with. Thankfully the sheet of paper inside hadn't torn. She was determined to find out why he'd done what he had for her parents, and fearing she already knew the answer.

Dear Ashley,
I can't believe you're really gone. I miss you so much.

She stopped. Checked the postmark date. Yes, it was the first letter. He'd written it when he'd been seventeen. And he'd really said that he missed her.

The new guy your parents hired is never on time, and I haven't been getting my breaks.

She snorted a laugh. That was more like the Ryan she knew.

Also, I've heard a couple of new jokes you might like. Here's one: Why can't a bankrupt cowboy complain? Because he's got no beef. Are you laughing? I bet you are. Anyway, I thought you might like to know your mom and dad are fine. A little sad, but we all are. When do you get leave? Hope it's at Christmas. I can't wait to see what you bring me.
With love,
Cowboy

Ashley painstakingly opened and flipped through several of the letters. They were all signed the same way. *With love, Cowboy.*

Maybe it was a good thing she hadn't read this first one when she was nineteen. She might've tossed it and never seen what he was telling her back then.

She read a few more, then found this one.

Dear Ashley,
It's your birthday, Sweet-Pea. I overheard your dad talking to you on the phone and shouted a greeting. Did you hear me? I don't know if your mom has told you, but your dad's Alzheimer's is getting worse. He's forgetting orders, forgot to approve the paychecks one week. It wasn't that big a deal for me, but one of the other guys was counting on cashing his that day.

She could guess who'd floated that employee a loan. Ryan.

And he's wandered off a couple times. I followed him into the library once, and he had no idea why he'd gone in there. I'm trying to help the best I can, but... You should come home. Take leave, if you can. Your mom needs the support. And maybe some changes need to be made around the store. I've been thinking about you a lot. I miss you. Your smile, the way you roll your eyes at me when I make a dumb joke. Stay safe!
With love,
Cowboy

There was one from two years back, about the lease.

Your parents have leased me the farm to run alfalfa. It won't make me a whole lot of money, but Joe and Mary need the income and it was sitting dormant.

In one envelope she found a collection of comic strips, clipped out of the local newspaper. And most of them made her chuckle.

Then there was one dated just before she'd lost her arm.

Dear Ashley,
I hate to be the bearer of bad news, but your mom's had a heart attack. The doctors said it was mild, and she should be fine in a few weeks. I didn't want you to worry, but I thought you should know. I'm taking care of the feed store and helping with your dad when I can, so there's not a lot to worry about there. Take care of yourself, I hope I get to see you sometime soon.
With love,
Cowboy

She read until her eyes drooped in the lamplight from exhaustion. She'd cried several times.

All this time, she'd thought Ryan was a flake. Working at the same place he'd started at in high school. She'd thought he'd been a college dropout. But the truth was, he'd been there for her parents when she couldn't. He'd pretty much single-handedly kept the store running, even changing his college plans to do so.

He'd brought her mom to her in the hospital when Ashley had been on the edge of survival.

He'd proved his love for her over and over, even when she hadn't been paying attention.

And she'd tossed it all back in his face tonight.

Deep in her heart, she'd known he wasn't capable of cheating her parents. That's not who he was. But she'd been scared of her feelings.

Scared that she loved him.

And sometimes the people you loved could hurt you. She'd learned that when she'd discovered she was adopted, discovered that her parents had been lying to her for her entire life. And though she'd forgiven them, now her dad had Alzheimer's. He was slipping away before her very eyes. Her mother, too, with the heart attack. Loving someone made you vulnerable. Ashley didn't like to be vulnerable.

But she also didn't like the thought of her life without Ryan in it.

He'd made himself invaluable to her. Like air.

She loved him. She loved the man she'd grown to know through the letters and through his actions since she'd been home. If she'd read the letters earlier, would her heart have already been his? She couldn't answer that. She hadn't been ready. Not until now.

The realization shook her.

She buried her head in her hand.

What was she going to do now?

Ryan arrived at the office just after dawn.

He hadn't slept more than a few winks last night. He'd been trying to figure out how everything had gone from a fun date night, celebrating his college graduation and rife with possibilities, to Ashley accusing him of taking advantage of her parents.

If she'd have thought it through, she would've seen that he'd done it all for her. Wouldn't she?

He finally gave up on sleep and headed to the store. Figured he'd work on the inventory reports due to the accountant later in the month.

He flipped on the office light and sank into the desk chair.

A lesser man might've called in sick today. Truth be told, he'd thought about it. What was he going to do when Ashley came in later? She'd been in every day since she'd returned.

He didn't want to face her, not now. He'd told her he loved her and been slapped down. Accused.

Would she fire him? If she learned the routines, she could run the place easily. What would he do then?

He scrubbed his hands down his face. Sighed.

When he reached to press the power button on the PC, he froze.

There was a plain white envelope lying across the computer keyboard. No name on it.

He picked it up and saw the flap wasn't sealed. What was this?

A single sheet of college-ruled paper slid out easily. He unfolded it to find a handwritten letter in what looked like a child's scrawl. As if a six-year-old had written it. Slanting letters, some falling off their lines.

Dear Cowboy,

His heart pounded in his ears when he read the salutation. He looked over his shoulder, but the hall outside his office was dark, and he couldn't see anyone back there. Everything was quiet.

I thought I could prove my bravery by going to war, but you've fought more battles than I have right here in Redbud Trails.

I thought you were irresponsible and incapable of being serious, but you've proven me wrong.

I thought you were a goofball, and maybe you are, but you're also

creative and smart and tenacious and caring.
    I never really thought you would steal from my parents. I was afraid.
Because I love you, too.
Will you forgive me?

    With love,
Your Soldier Girl

His heart had gone from *pounding* to *overdrive*. Adrenaline pumped through his veins so that his hands shook as he folded the letter and slid it back into the envelope.

He had to find Ashley. It was early, and none of the other employees were scheduled to arrive for at least another hour. He could go to her.

He got to his feet.

A noise in the hallway. He turned, and there she was. Hanging back in the darkness, unsure. Was Atlas with her, or was she alone?

"I saw your truck pass the house," she said softly. "Did you read my letter?"

He lifted it so she could see. "I was a little afraid it might be a pink slip."

She winced slightly. "So you"—she cleared her throat— "didn't read it?"

"I read it."

Her hand flexed at her side, the only sign of her agitation. "I read yours, too. Finally. And...I'm sorry."

He couldn't hold back any longer. He rounded his desk and crossed the small office to reach her, then hauled her into his arms, burying his face in the crown of her hair. "I didn't mean to keep anything from you. At first, I barely gave the lease a thought. I'd written to you about it..."

She shook her head, her nose and chin brushing against his chest with the motion. "It doesn't matter. I knew—deep down, I knew that there was no way you were cheating them. After everything you've done..."

Her voice sounded teary, and he tipped her head up. He

kissed her deeply, trying to communicate that his feelings hadn't changed. She sighed against his mouth and he ended the kiss, but he couldn't let her go. He placed a kiss on her cheek and held her close, giving them both the chance to catch their breaths.

"Don't misunderstand," he said between pants. "I would've been here for Joe and Mary regardless of your feelings. My dad left a long time ago, and your parents are like family."

She moved back slightly but didn't try to leave his embrace. "I don't know what I'm doing here yet. My dad, he needs a lot of care. And I've missed so much with my mom. I'm still finding out who I am. Even though you...you love me," her voice squeaked on the words, and he kissed her again, kissed her until she was melting in his arms.

He tucked her head beneath his chin. "I love you," he said softly, because his mouth was so close to her ear. "I love you whatever happens. With your dad. With what you decide to do with your life."

He lowered his mouth a minuscule amount closer to her ear. "And I'd really like to hear you say it back to me."

He felt more than saw her smile widen against the side of his jaw. For a moment, he wondered if she would torment him, make him wait, but she whispered, "I love you."

"I liked your letter," he whispered back.

"Good. It took me about as long to write it as it took to read all of yours."

Knowing how difficult it had been for her to write it with her left hand made him treasure the effort even more.

"We don't have to have everything figured out right now," he said against her cheek, slowly making his way back to her lips.

"That sounds like a Ryan thing to say," she murmured, and he kissed her again. She broke away slightly to say, "But I'm game to try."

MISTLETOE COWBOY

CHAPTER ONE

"Can I get you a cappuccino? Latte?"

The girl behind the drive-thru window of the Coffee Hut—a small shack in the superstore parking lot on the edge of town—smiled at him, and Justin Michaels had to bite back a goofy smile.

"Just coffee. Black."

Her shiny brown ponytail bobbed, and strands of inky dark hair clung to her neck as she turned to pick up a cardboard mug.

"You sure?" She shot him a coquettish look over her shoulder, a glimpse of her honey-brown eyes from beneath her eyelashes.

"Yep."

It was their usual routine.

Her name was Valri. He knew it because he'd seen her nametag the first time he'd come. He had a love affair with coffee and usually stopped by once a day. Or twice.

"Is that—are you *flirting* with her?"

Justin kept his eyes on the gravel parking lot out of the truck's front windshield and worked at not reacting to his sister-in-law's hissed words from the passenger seat. The bright October sunshine made him squint, made his head pound—or maybe it was Haley's shock.

He couldn't tell if she were appalled or excited.

With one wrist dangling over the top of the steering wheel, he let the other arm rest across the bench seat-back. Relaxed. Like he hadn't a care in the world.

Haley Michaels née Carston had been married to his brother for all of a month and made Maddox happier than Justin had ever seen his brother.

Justin was happy for Maddox. He just wanted Haley to quit trying to set him up. With her friends. A gal from church. And a random chick from the grocery store.

He was tired of it. He wasn't in any place to be dating right now.

Plus, he really didn't want Valri the coffee shop girl to hear Haley. Much as he tried not to notice these things, there was no way to overlook it—Valri was hot.

This coffee-thing, this was just their routine. A harmless one. Maybe they flirted when he visited the Coffee Hut. But he never did anything about it.

She didn't wear a wedding ring. He'd checked that the first time he'd driven through.

But she was young. With her hair pulled back in a long brown ponytail and no makeup hiding the adorable freckles across her nose, she could be anywhere from sixteen to twenty.

And although he was only twenty-seven, he felt much older.

Hobbling around like an old man and sometimes relying on a cane to work the kinks out in the morning did nothing to make a man feel young.

His doctors told him he was lucky to walk at all after his career-ending injury, but most days he didn't feel lucky.

Except for the ten minutes that he interacted with Valri-the-coffee-girl. When she smiled at him, he felt *everything*.

"Here you go," Valri said, extending his coffee through the hut's drive-thru window. And yep, her full-wattage smile made his stomach kick like one of the bulls he used to challenge in the arena.

This was why he had never pursued anything with her. That zing of attraction between them was strong. Maybe too strong.

He would be toxic for a girl like that, young and innocent. Between his ugly past and his present, daily struggles, there was no room for dating.

At least that's what he told himself.

Valri North handed the handsome cowboy his tall coffee, brushing his fingertips accidentally—or maybe not so accidentally. She loved the feeling of those sparks skittering up her arm and down her spine. No shot of espresso could replicate that.

He always paid in cash, or she would've looked at his debit card to learn his name.

Shameful, but a girl had to do what a girl had to do to feed her dreams. Those dreams had to get her through four years of med school and a residency. And a handsome cowboy in a battered truck—he was enough to fuel plenty of dreams. The hint of stubble at his jaw made him look slightly disreputable. Those brown curls poking out from beneath the brim of his Stetson… yeah, he'd do.

She'd given some thought to asking him out. She saw him almost every day at the Coffee Hut. One or two dates wouldn't be serious and would give her fodder for the G-rated fantasies that were her only escape. If only she could be like some of her classmates, who dated without regard to the consequences—to their hearts and their grades. She'd been labeled a nerd in second grade, and the older she got, the more she believed it.

She hadn't been on a date since her sixteenth birthday four years ago. And she was happy with that. Wasn't she? She had plans for her future. Big plans. Plans that mattered.

She looked back at the cowboy, who was watching with lifted eyebrows.

She shook off the errant thoughts and looked beyond the handsome cowboy to the woman sitting beside him. Another reason to keep her distance. "Are you sure your girlfriend doesn't want something?"

He choked, and the pretty woman with auburn hair in the passenger seat let out a peal of laughter. She clapped her hands in front of her, and Valri got a flash of a brilliant diamond on the woman's finger.

Fiancée?

The bottom dropped out of Valri's stomach.

"Don't tell your brother. He'll be furious with us both."

She could see the strain in his smile by the lines at the corner of his eyes. "My *sister-in-law* doesn't need any caffeine to feed her orneriness. But thanks."

He wasn't engaged. Or at least, he wasn't engaged to the woman in the truck.

The relief Valri felt was unexpected, and welcome.

His smile was powerful, the flash of white teeth under his tan, the lines around his mouth that eased into the expression.

Do you want to go out sometime? But the words stuck, just behind her teeth.

"I'll see you tomorrow?" she asked.

"You always do."

He gave a little wave before his big hand settled on the steering wheel, and then he was gone.

It was just as well. She was too busy and had too many plans to be distracted by a handsome cowboy. It was a pipe dream for her, wasn't it?

She had other things to focus on. Her nightmare started tonight at six-thirty. She had roughly two semesters left in her undergrad and had only now gotten up the guts to take the class she was most dreading.

Not Anatomy, complete with cadaver lab. That had been a breeze.

Comm 2. Speech class.

The eight-week, concentrated course had been the only one she could fit it into her course load. And tonight was the night.

No turning back.

She had to pull a B to keep up her GPA, but an A would be better. Med schools didn't accept slackers, and she wanted into the best school in the state.

The med school in Oklahoma City was close enough to home that she might be able to help out her parents on the weekends. She didn't want to move out of state, but if she had to, she would. She was prepared to do whatever it took to become a doctor. It was her calling.

She hoped her parents and younger siblings were ready as well.

She sighed as she let her eyes linger on the state road where the cowboy's truck had disappeared in a plume of gravel dust.

It was better this way. She would enjoy the five minutes of dreaming that her schedule allowed, and focus on what mattered. Like she always did.

CHAPTER TWO

Later that night, Justin slouched in the second-furthest seat on the last row of the university classroom. The small state university was a forty-minute drive from Redbud Trails, and he was working laboriously through several classes. This was all Haley's fault. She'd convinced him he needed direction in his life. Problem was, he still didn't have it, despite her hopes.

At least the classes had gotten him off his butt, out of his late dad's awful recliner, and back to real life.

Outside the window, the foliage on the trees planted next to the building had turned gold and orange, and the October breeze rustled the few remaining leaves as the setting sun spread pink fingers across the sky. He was most definitely a non-traditional student, coming back to school at his age, and the night classes fit into his part-time work schedule.

His legs stretched out in front of the desk that was too small. Most were, though, because of his six-foot-two inch stature, and also because of his injury—a broken pelvis—and the lingering discomfort he suffered.

The eighteen-year-old gal next to him had been trying to catch his eye since he'd sat down. The classroom was amphitheater-style, and he hadn't wanted to battle the stairs every class period, or he might've moved closer to the front—and away from the girl—before the prof had started talking.

The classroom was close to full. There were probably forty kids—kids to him, at least—listening attentively to the professor's first-night welcome. They were probably five minutes in when the door behind him opened with an audible squeak. There was an empty seat on Justin's left, and he felt the latecomer approach.

A backpack shielded the girl's face, but as she stepped over the guy to Justin's right, it slipped off her shoulder and almost clocked him in the head. Would have, if he hadn't ducked.

He leaned away from the girl and was about to glare at her when he saw it was Valri from the Coffee Hut.

Heat slipped up the back of his neck. He tried to get his feet out of her way, but she stepped at the same time and got tangled in his boots.

She let out a strangled *"Eep!"* and landed in the seat next to him with a grunt. Her backpack *thunked* against the desk. How many textbooks did she have in there?

He got a whiff of a sweet, flowery perfume and under that, a strong scent of coffee that had him breathing in deep.

"Sorry," he muttered.

And then he realized the professor had gone ominously silent. A glance at the front of the room showed the man staring sternly in their direction.

"Thank you for joining us, Miss…?"

"North. Valri North. I'm sorry I'm late, sir."

The prof smiled, but it looked more like a sneer. "I was just telling the class that three tardies will earn you an absence. Three absences and you will fail the class. I don't like my class being disrupted. It's disrespectful to me and to your fellow students."

She muttered something beneath her breath, then smiled tightly and said, "I apologize."

"Harsh," Justin said under his breath.

She had a hand inside her backpack and shot a glance at him. Her eyes were narrowed and her lips turned down in a frown, but when her eyes slid to his face, they widened, her frown lifted.

"Cowboy," she hissed in surprise.

"Hey, Coffee Shop."

Someone from her other side cleared his throat, and she blushed, turned that direction, and accepted a stack of syllabi.

Their fingers brushed as she handed Justin the papers and, just like that morning at the Coffee Hut, he felt a tingle of attraction zip through him.

Just after he passed the syllabi to the blonde on his right, the last person in their row, a seating chart followed. He scribbled his name in the square that lined up with the chair he was sitting in and then swallowed hard when his eyes fell on the curly, feminine *Vahi North* in the square next to his.

He was going to have to sit next to her for the entire eight weeks? Crap.

The stadium-style seating was a problem. To get to the front of the class, he would have to wrangle himself down the flight of stairs, which would be a challenge with his limited mobility.

He could always drop the class. But Haley had pushed him to not give up on himself. Was it giving up to try and avoid complete public humiliation?

This really sucked.

She was going to spend eight weeks next to the cowboy. Justin Michaels. She'd surreptitiously watched him scrawl his name on the seating chart. Maybe it wasn't polite but she'd waited so long to learn his name, she wasn't going to miss her chance.

Having the handsome cowboy in her class was going to be a nightmare. Of all the people to have to witness her humiliation, it had to be someone she found incredibly attractive.

And that on top of the professor's grumpy attitude. It wasn't her fault she'd been tardy. She hated being late.

But she hated being the center of attention more, and he'd focused every eye in the classroom to her.

This was why she had left this particular class until she was well into her undergrad degree. She hated the thought of speaking in front of anyone. She could deal with all kinds of blood and gore—and frequently did at the free clinic where she volunteered—but speaking in front of her peers? The thought of it was enough to make her vomit.

She flipped to the second page of the syllabus and used a red pen to circle the three dates she was dreading most on the schedule: the three oral presentations she would have to deliver.

And she was paying enough attention to hear the professor say, "…you will be graded solely on three oral examinations."

Her heart pulsed in her throat.

Someone raised a hand. "There's no written test? No final exam?"

"Your final speech *is* your final exam."

Was she imagining that unholy, gleeful gleam in the professor's eyes? Maybe it was the glare of the overhead lights on his glasses. Or maybe not.

Another hand went up and a tremulous voice asked, "What about extra credit?"

"I was getting to that."

Valri flipped to the last page of the syllabus and circled the paragraph under the heading *EXTRA CREDIT* with her red pen. If she were going to be graded only on her speaking ability, she was going to need all the help she could get.

Her GPA wouldn't handle anything less than a B in this class. She had to pass with a decent grade or risk not getting into her top choice for med school.

She was exhausted. She'd worked from five a.m. to lunchtime at the Coffee Hut, then rushed to the free clinic to work through her volunteer hours. Her mom had had to work a nursing shift at the hospital, leaving Valri to collect her younger siblings from school and make sure they'd gotten dinner. She'd rushed out of the house at the same time her dad had rushed in, exhausted from his job running the family hardware store.

Her stomach growled loudly, reminding her she'd forgotten the Tupperware containing her own supper. She'd been in a hurry to make it to the campus bookstore before it closed, because she hadn't had a spare moment to get up here and buy her book before now.

The cowboy's head tilted in her direction. Her cheeks flamed, and she kept her eyes on the paper on her desk.

Even though she was on high alert from sitting next to the cowboy of her daydreams, after long minutes of the professor's droning voice, she could barely keep her eyes open. It wasn't until he declared they would be doing an icebreaker exercise that she came back to herself with a start.

There were an odd number of students in their row, and the professor assigned her with Justin and the bleached-blonde next to him. They had to discover three interesting things about their partners and then reveal them to the rest of the class.

As the noise in the class ratcheted up, she turned in her seat, clenching her teeth in what she hoped was a semblance of a smile. She hated exercises like this. It wasn't that she was shy—she wasn't—but she was in university for one reason: to get to med school. She didn't see why she had to stand up in front of the entire class to introduce someone when she was here simply to learn.

She looked up to see the cowboy's eyes on her. On his other side, the blonde had scooted her chair closer than was strictly necessary.

"Hi, I'm Brandi!"

The blonde hadn't spared one glance for Valri. Her entire focus was on the cowboy between them.

Something twisted inside Valri's stomach. Probably hunger pangs. It had to be.

"Justin Michaels." He glanced over at the blonde, and she lit up, squealing behind the hand she held over her mouth.

She clasped both hands beneath her chin. "Oh, I knew it was you the instant I saw you! I followed your career—well, my older brother did—and I've seen all your commercials. This is so exciting to be in class with someone famous!"

Was it her, or had the tips of the cowboy's ears turned red? He shrugged, his eyes focused on the desk in front of him.

"I'm not really famous," he muttered.

"Sure you are!" Brandi chirped.

"Famous for what?" Valri hadn't meant to speak aloud, but apparently she had, because both of their heads turned toward her.

The blonde wore an expression of horror mixed with irritation, while the cowboy met her gaze evenly. It was hard not to look down with the intensity of those ice-blue eyes focused right at her.

Brandi's pink-tipped nails curled over the cowboy's shoulder. "Justin is a bull rider," she said, her voice and manner almost proprietary.

"*Was* a bull rider."

Was a bull rider.

Justin hadn't meant his words to come out with such a final, bitter ring to them, but he couldn't help that now.

How unlucky could he be that the blonde had recognized him? And did she have to put so much emphasis on the *older brother* who had followed his career?

What little fame he'd garnered from his bull riding days had imploded two-and-a-half years ago when his career had tanked. Everyone in Redbud Trails knew who he was, and most were kind enough to not mention his rodeo career. Here at the university, it was the luck of the draw whether or not he would be recognized.

And this rodeo-bunny-wannabe had to bring up his failed career.

In front of Valri, who for some unknown reason, he actually wanted to impress.

Valri's latte-colored eyes assessed him steadily as he shrugged. Conveniently, Brandi's hand fell away from his shoulder.

"And you are…?" he said, desperate for the focus to come off of him.

"Valri North."

He stuck out his hand and enveloped her smaller, cool one. "Nice to meet you, Valri."

She smiled, a real smile. Guileless. Kind.

He had to swallow hard.

"So should we interview each other?" Brandi's voice intruded on the moment that had seemed almost private. He glanced at her, realizing he'd almost turned his shoulder on her.

She was motioning between herself and him, as if she hadn't even noticed Valri's presence.

"That would leave out Valri, wouldn't it?"

He saw the beginnings of a pout in the downturned corners of her lips, and he rushed on to forestall it.

"How about Brandi can interview me, Valri can interview Brandi, and I'll interview Valri. Does that work?"

Brandi seemed to accept the plan with a tight smile and a small huff of air.

Valri flipped open a notebook and poised her pen over the top as if eager to take notes.

He stretched back in his chair, letting its front legs come off the floor. Pretended like it didn't bother him to have to open up to two virtual strangers. Nope, didn't bother him in the least.

Yeah, right.

"So… three things?" He interlocked the fingers of both hands behind his head, trying to look relaxed. "I'm a *former* bull rider," he said with a nod to Brandi, who looked like she was soaking up every single word he said. Great. He'd have to figure out a way to avoid her over the next eight weeks.

"I love ice cream," he went on. It was a good thing too, with his niece Livy running her own gourmet ice cream business. He, his brother, Maddox, and his cousin, Ryan would likely be thirty pounds overweight if they didn't work it off doing manual labor to keep the family farm operational.

He continued, "And I love Christmas." Also true.

Brandi wrinkled her nose. "Those are the most interesting things about you?"

"Yup." The most interesting things he was willing to share with her, a virtual stranger-slash-bunny.

"Shouldn't you mention you're a coffee aficionado?" Valri whispered.

His eyes darted to her. She was grinning, a private grin, one that he wanted to answer.

There was danger in those brown eyes, that sweet smile. And yet he couldn't resist answering her. "Can you be an aficionado if you've never tried anything but black?"

"What?" Brandi asked, clearly lost.

He turned back to her and shook his head.

The blonde bunny looked like she wanted to say something else, probably ask if he were single. Her mouth even parted, but then Valri broke in. "We only have five minutes left to complete the assignment. Brandi, why don't you go next?"

The blonde huffed, but Valri didn't look like she'd be swayed. She was maybe, what…? A year older than Brandi at the most? But there was something different about her. Something serious, older than her years, behind those eyes.

Whatever it was, it drew him. He locked those feelings down, tied them off as tight as he used to tie his grip hand when he was on the back of a bull.

"I'm a Taurus. I was on the cheer squad all four years of high school." She delivered that with a quirk of her head. "And I was prom queen."

Valri's dutifully made notes, but he saw the corner of her mouth quirking.

Was she thinking the same thing he was? That Bunny Brandi was living in the past, still riding on high school successes?

It made him feel old. And a little sorry for her. He'd learned the hard way that living in the past was a surefire way to miss out on the present.

He heard Brandi's intake of air, as if she were going to throw herself into the conversation again.

He jumped in before she could. "All right, Valri. What are the three most interesting things about you?"

A slight pink tinged her cheeks, and her eyes flicked down to her desk. "I'm the third of ten children in my family."

"Wow." He hadn't meant to speak aloud, but her chin came up, her eyes flashing to him.

"By credit hours, I'm a junior. And I'm going to be a doctor."

She said it with such calm certainty, he was momentarily envious.

He heard her stomach gurgle again, and his curiosity was piqued. She was the most interesting person he'd met in a long time—mostly because he'd purposely avoided situations like this. He tended to stay away from girls that had *settle down with me* written all over them. And even though she was chasing an ambitious dream, he'd place money on Valri being married before she graduated med school. Some lucky guy was going to snatch her up.

It just couldn't be him.

The prof called the class back to order, and the students on the first row started the introductions. Justin settled his chair with all four legs back on the floor and shifted slightly when the constant ache in his pelvis became too sharp.

When it was his turn to stand up with Brandi and Valri, he was careful to push up from the desk with his arms, surreptitiously steadying himself until he could get his legs beneath him.

Maybe it was egotistical, but Valri had always seen him sitting in his truck. She didn't know he limped like a gimpy old man or that sometimes his legs didn't want to hold him up. And he didn't want her to witness him fall on his face tonight.

There'd been chemistry between them. He didn't want to watch it disappear when she realized how broken he was.

CHAPTER THREE

Justin kicked his booted feet out of the way as Valri rushed into class, with wisps of her dark hanging down into her face. She set that back-breaking load of books on her desk with a thunk and collapsed into her seat.

"Three minutes to spare," he said.

She folded her arms over the backpack and lowered her head onto them with a groan, burying her face so he couldn't see it. Since the first night, she hadn't been officially late, though she'd rushed into class almost every time.

"I can't do this," she said, her voice muffled by her sweatshirt.

"What, give your speech?"

Two weeks into the class and the first presentation was due. He'd watched the first half of the class give their three-minute speeches during the last class period. He'd been bored to tears—except when he was biting back laughter. The kids were green, all of them.

None of them had been stepped on by the two-and-a-half ton bull of *life*, not like Justin had.

He pushed the wrapped deli sandwich from his desk onto Valri's.

She looked up at the rattle of paper, then looked at him, tilting her head to the side.

"Finally got tired of hearing your stomach growl all during class."

She turned a pretty shade of rose. "I'm sorry."

"Don't be," he said. "Seems like you're always rushing in at the last minute."

Brandi slurped her drink, setting the disposable cup on the corner of her desk, just inches from the matching cup in front of him.

"We were at Jay's Deli before class. You should stop by sometime," Brandi said.

He gritted his teeth. The blonde made it look as if they'd been there together. Sure, they'd both been there, but only because she'd followed him in to the deli and then stood too close in line. He'd rebuffed her to the point of near-rudeness so he could eat his sandwich alone.

Valri's eyes flicked between the two of them. She nodded, but her earlier smile had faded. "Thanks."

She tucked the sandwich into the top of her backpack, exchanging it for a stack of three-by-five cards. Her hands were shaking.

"Aren't you going to eat it?"

"Not until after I do my speech. I already feel nauseous."

She did look a little green.

"You're nervous?"

"Aren't you?"

"I'm not." Brandi inserted herself into the conversation again. She leaned forward, her eyes locked on Justin. "I bet when you've faced down a two-thousand-pound animal, public speaking seems pretty boring."

With Brandi leaning toward him like that, there was nowhere to go. It was like being pinned to the arena railing with an angry animal and no rodeo clown to save your life. Sorta.

He leaned toward Valri. Their eyes met and caught for a long second before the professor began the class. She turned to face the front of the classroom.

Public speaking might not be the adrenaline rush he'd experienced on the back of a bull, but there was nothing boring about Valri. It was why he'd done his best not to notice her for the first two weeks of class, at least not outside polite greetings and goodbyes.

What had possessed him to bring her a sandwich tonight?

That definitely showed he'd noticed her. And that he liked her.

That was dangerous. Not only was he a *has-been*, but with his history, he was no good for someone like Valri. He doubted she would even give him the time of day if she knew about his womanizing days. Or worse, the addiction he'd fought—and still fought—after his injury.

He'd keep his secrets, pretend that being friendly in class was enough for him when he really wanted more. He wanted to know her.

He probably cared what she thought a little too much, because he'd always dawdled gathering up his things after class, sometimes even talking to Brandi, though he tried to talk to the jock one seat in front of him when he could.

All because he didn't want Valri to see him limp out of the classroom.

Stupid pride.

Tonight it was all going up in flames, because he was going to have to stand up and walk down the stadium-style stairs to the front of the classroom.

And try not to fall on his face.

The prof had been calling students in alphabetical order, so Justin's name was called soon.

He pushed out from the desk and ambled down the aisle toward the stairs. How many times had he done something similar on the rodeo circuit? Pretended he was fine before a ride, when in reality, he'd been full of aches and pains? Once he'd even ridden with a broken wrist.

This was just like that. Except not.

Valri watched the long-legged cowboy limp down the stairs toward the podium. For a moment, the anxiety that plagued her was relegated to the back burner as she guessed what possible injury he might have.

Why hadn't she seen him limp before? Because he always remained seated after class, making friends and flirting.

He'd never flirted with her.

She'd noticed, of course, because something had passed between them that first night. He didn't seem to really be interested in Brandi. She couldn't put her finger on it, but when he flirted with the other girl, something felt *off*. Like he was going through the motions. Like his heart wasn't really in it.

She looked at the sandwich sticking out of her backpack. That gesture had clogged her throat with emotion.

Her family was great. She loved the big, noisy bunch. But someone constantly needed something. Homework help. Supper. A ride to band practice.

Having someone look after her was a nice surprise. A shocking surprise.

Justin lay his single sheet of notebook paper on the podium and looked up at the audience. He spoke with a calm, self-assured presence, telling the class about the benefits of small business ownership, using several anecdotes about his niece and her ice cream.

He kept looking at her. Oh, she knew she was probably imagining it, but every time his eyes roved the seated students, his gaze seemed to settle on her.

The corner of his mouth turned up in a smile, as if they were sharing a secret.

Maybe she wasn't imagining it, because a girl seated in the row in front of her craned her neck back and looked right at Valri.

Her face burned. Like she hadn't been nervous enough.

Thankfully, his three minutes and the weird looks ended, and he slowly made his way back up to their row and slouched in his chair.

Two students separated him and Valri alphabetically. Six minutes...five now before she had to stand up in front of everyone.

Her stomach gurgled, and not in an *I'm hungry* kind of way. She pressed a trembling hand into her gut, but it didn't help. Her other hand tapped on her notes. The slight noise just agitated her further, but she couldn't seem to stop.

"Don't worry."

Justin leaned toward her, his wide hand settling on the edge of her desk.

She couldn't even speak to tell him to be quiet. Her stupid fingers tapped faster.

"Everyone is nervous," he whispered.

She wasn't one to talk in class—always afraid of getting in trouble. But she hissed, "You weren't."

"Sure I was. Why do you think I kept looking at you? Prettiest girl in the room distracted me enough that I got over it."

He was lying. He had to be. She definitely wasn't the prettiest girl in this class. She wasn't even wearing makeup.

But then his hand closed over hers, stilling her fingers from tapping.

His hand was warm. Heat slid up her arm and then flamed into her face.

He'd said she was the prettiest girl in the room. What if he hadn't been kidding?

Belatedly, she registered her name being called. She jerked her head up to see the professor staring at her with a hard look in his eyes.

Justin let go of her hand, and she stumbled up from the desk.

Somehow she made it down the stairs.

And then as she stepped off the last step, her trembling fingers dropped the index cards.

There was an audible gasp from someone on the front row.

Fire streaked through her, burning up her neck and face as she knelt to gather them up.

There were twenty cards, and as she held the jumble in her violently shaking hands, she stepped behind the podium.

She tried to sort them, but somehow her vision had blurred.

The professor cleared his throat.

Her mind was completely blank. She was going to bomb

this speech.

"The usual?"

The next morning, Justin sat in his truck at the Coffee Hut, his breath fogging the space between his truck and the drive-up window. It was colder than usual for late-October in Oklahoma.

Valri's usual sparkle was missing, her greeting subdued. He could tell she was still upset about what had happened last night with her presentation.

Last night she'd trudged back up the stairs with her shoulders hunched and had practically ran out the room at the end of the class period. He'd seen the tears pooled in her eyes.

Obviously, it was still on her mind.

"I was thinking about trying one of those caramel what's-see-do-hickeys."

She'd already taken a cardboard cup from the stack. She turned back toward the window in shock. "A macchiato? You really want to try one?"

He let the corners of his mouth tip up. "Nope."

She rolled her eyes, but her shoulders had lifted slightly.

"You weren't that bad," he said.

She shot him a scathing, skeptical look. "I was horrible."

It hadn't been *that* bad. She'd started out shaky, her voice trembling and too quiet, but then she'd found her feet and finished fairly strong.

"Some of the other kids messed up, too," he offered, wanting to console her. "Brandi didn't do so hot—"

"Brandi doesn't want to be a doctor."

He laughed, but she was as steamed as the coffee that gurgled in the machine in front of her.

What was the big deal? This was just one part of the grade. And even if she had to retake the class, which he thought was very doubtful, it wasn't that big a deal, was it?

"Flubbing one presentation isn't going to ruin your entire academic career."

She just shook her head, passing his black coffee through

the window. When their fingers tangled and he would have normally backed off, he grasped them.

Her eyes flew to his, and the hint of vulnerability in their depths hit him like a punch in the guts. "It's going to be all right."

She pushed the coffee cup into his hand and drew back, then blew a breath upward to dislodge a wisp of hair that had stuck to her forehead. She shook her head slightly. "I wish I could believe you, but I'm afraid this is going to mess up my plans."

He let his eyebrows rise slightly. "You've got a master plan, huh?"

She looked slightly sheepish, but when she spoke it was with a distinctly determined air. "The plan is to apply to med school this spring. If my GPA tanks because of this class, I won't get into the school I want."

"I doubt your GPA will *tank* if you make a C for Comm 2."

She shrugged, now avoiding his gaze. "I need to pull a B or better. I don't know if I can recover from last night's disaster."

He didn't know what to say. The longer this conversation went on, the more it ventured into *friend* territory. And he needed to keep her in the acquaintance zone. *Friend* was only one step removed from *dating*, and that was a place he definitely couldn't go.

But then she hiked her chin. "I'm going to pull my grade up," she said firmly. "And I'm going to follow the plan."

He had to smile at her insistence.

But later, long after he'd driven off and was back at the farm, when he was repairing a torn section of barbed-wire fence, he couldn't shake the memory of her passion and determination.

What was that like, having such a firm destination for your life?

He didn't know what he would be doing next week, other than more of the same. He had no idea what he wanted out of life.

Except for more time with her—the one thing he couldn't

have.

Valri was like one of the bright red cardinals that soared out of the woods behind the barn. She was on an upward trajectory, spreading her wings and flying.

And he was grounded. Too afraid to take a risk again, too afraid that his past was going to catch up with him. What if he hit rock bottom again? He didn't know if he had the strength to pull himself up all over again.

CHAPTER FOUR

"You're not dressed."

Justin's shoulders tensed at Brandi's half-whining tone as the classroom began to fill with students and noise. He glanced up and found she was wearing a banana-colored, princess-style dress with a huge, puffy skirt. She had a tiara in her hair, which had been wrapped into a bun.

He looked down at his T-shirt and faded jeans. "I'm dressed."

"You're not dressed *up*," Brandi said, pushing the issue. When she sat down, her dress was all up in his space, pressing against his jeans.

Valri moved past him, taking her seat a few minutes earlier than usual. He saw her lips twitching with a grin.

She was wearing regular clothes, a sweatshirt and jeans, but had painted a pink nose and black whiskers on her face, which matched nicely with the bunny ears perched on top of her head.

He grabbed his Stetson off his desk and smashed it on his head. "There. I'm a rodeo cowboy."

"*Former*," Valri murmured from beside him.

And he found himself grinning a wide, silly grin. One that she returned.

"Happy Halloween," she said softly, depositing a Coffee Hut paper coffee cup and cardboard wrapper on one corner of his desk.

"Back atcha." He placed a wrapped sandwich and small tub of soup on hers. "You didn't have to bring me anything."

"Neither did you, but that hasn't stopped you yet. Thanks." She tipped the soup at him before raising it to her lips and sipping straight from the bowl.

He'd made a habit of bringing her something to eat since the night of her first failed speech. She'd been so disappointed that night, it seemed the least he could do. His gestures had nothing to do with the smile she gave him now.

They usually only had a couple of minutes together—with Brandi always there—before class started, but he'd learned a lot about her during those minutes.

She was smart. He'd seen the advanced science textbooks in her backpack and learned she was serious about becoming a doctor. She'd shared that she volunteered several hours a week in a free clinic. He couldn't figure how she got everything done.

He picked up the coffee and took a sip. He wrinkled his nose and shoved it away from him on the very corner of his desk. "What was that?"

She doubled over giggling, even though she had a mouthful of sandwich. She chewed and swallowed. "Pumpkin spice. For the holidays."

"Why would you do that to me?"

"You never try anything other than *coffee, black*," she said in a creditable impression of him.

He raised his brows, and her lips twitched.

She reached behind her and traded the pumpkin crap for another, identical cup. "Okay, it was a Halloween prank."

He took it, leaving one skeptical brow raised at her. He sniffed the opening and was rewarded with a whiff of strong, plain coffee.

He sipped it gingerly. "Aaah, sweet nectar."

She shook her head, taking another big bite of sandwich. She swallowed. "How many cups of coffee do you consume, anyway?"

"Daily? Five or six."

"That's a lot of caffeine, buster."

"Says the coffee shop girl."

"Says a future doctor," she corrected.

Indeed. And maybe it was too much, but he needed it. Or that's what it felt like. If he had to have one vice, he'd rather it be coffee than the pain meds he'd relied on to get through those dark days after he'd lost everything.

Nope, he wasn't going to think about that. He sipped his coffee and then set it down. "I've been trying to figure something out."

She hummed something that might've been *"What?"* over her next mouthful. It gave him a deep, intense joy to see her enjoying his gift.

"How old are you? You said that first night you were a junior but..."

He let his voice trail off when she got a peculiar expression on her face.

She swallowed and took a sip of the pumpkin coffee. There was something intimate in knowing his lips had been on that same spot a minute ago.

He swallowed hard.

"But..."

He'd nearly forgotten what he'd been saying and floundered.

"But I'm too young to be a junior?" she asked.

There was an edge to her voice that hadn't been there before.

"I graduated high school at sixteen and a half. Between med school and residency, I have a lot of school ahead of me."

"So you started early?"

She nodded. "Why not? I know my path."

It was the thing he envied most about her. She knew what she wanted out of life, and she wasn't afraid to chase after it.

He'd been like that. Before. Chasing his dreams of being a champion and having the financial freedom that had seemed so unattainable when he'd been a kid.

Now he was listless. A ship without a rudder. A man without a goal.

The prof started class, and at the break, Brandi tipped her

head coquettishly at him. "There's a Halloween party later tonight at one of the frat houses. Do you want to go? With me?"

Three years ago, he would have accepted her invitation and whatever else she offered him. He would have had no thought for consequences. Only for fun.

But he smiled a little and tried to let her down easy. "No, thanks."

Valri stayed in her seat, finishing the notes she was frantically scribbling.

He didn't think she was paying any attention, but after Brandi huffed away, Valri kept her head down and asked, "Why didn't you go out with her?"

"She's too young for me."

He'd meant the words to be flippant, but she didn't look up. He could see pink filling her cheeks.

Had she been fishing? If she had, did that mean she'd thought about dating him herself?

The thought both elated him and gave him pause.

For her sake, he needed to keep his distance.

Valri rubbed her sand-filled eyes. She was the only one awake and felt like the clock was judging her as it flipped past one a.m.

She had to be at work in four hours. And she was supposed to be writing the last two paragraphs of a research paper for her biochem class, but instead she had an online video site open.

And she couldn't look away from the horrific images of Justin falling from the back of a huge brown bull. And then being stepped on.

She'd been curious about how he'd been injured. She'd followed a link on the page and surfed through several follow up stories. It had been a career-ending injury. He'd never ridden a bull again. And she knew he still limped. Based on the way she'd caught him wincing a few times, she knew it still hurt.

She'd found herself back on the original video, watching his injury over and over again, watching the paramedics rush onto the scene, watching them load Justin onto a stretcher and take him out of the arena, his face etched with intense pain.

She'd originally gone to the site to look up his endorsements. Brandi talked about them in class often enough, and Valri couldn't help wondering. There had been commercials of him wearing a well-known brand of cowboy jeans, throwing hay bales into the back of a pickup truck.

The man had a nice backside.

But Valri was drawn to his pain.

What drove a man to choose bull riding as a career path? There was no doubt he was good at it. There had been videos of many successful rides, lists of purses he'd won.

What drove him now? Seemed he didn't date. Tonight wasn't the first time she'd overheard Brandi ask him out.

And yet... he brought *Valri* supper every class period.

She'd thought about him a lot. Even before their class, when he'd only been a face to serve at the Coffee Hut, she'd found her thoughts drawn to him. And now, Justin was never far from her mind.

She'd almost gotten up the nerve to ask him out herself. But it hadn't mattered, because if he thought Brandi was too young for him, then surely he'd think Valri was, too.

She'd chickened out.

But she was still here, online, watching videos of the enigmatic cowboy when she should be studying.

He was such a contradiction. Kind when he brought her food since she didn't usually have time to eat supper. Distant when she attempted to get personal in conversation.

Not that she should be surprised. She wasn't anything special. Third of ten children, her best qualities were her ambition and her family loyalty.

But that wasn't anything special. Her family was the opposite of well-off.

Why would someone like him be interested in a nerd like her?

CHAPTER FIVE

An extreme cold front blew in over the weekend and a few campus emails speculated about the possibility of class being cancelled. It wasn't.

Valri watched the snow falling harder and harder out the classroom windows and then, *finally*, the Comm 2 professor let them out of class early.

She was about to rush out the back door when he called her to the front of the class to talk about some questions she'd emailed him about the extra credit project. When she finally made her way to the commuter parking lot, it was deserted except for her snow-crusted blue Honda sedan.

Snow buffeted her, battering her body. She'd loaned her younger sister her heavy winter coat, and her leather jacket wasn't much protection against the frigid wind. She'd forgotten a scarf and gloves.

The only thing she dreaded more than driving through this mess for an hour—that could easily turn into two—was cleaning all that snow off her car. But what choice did she have?

And then as she approached, she noticed her car was leaning to one side. It hadn't been like that when she left it to go inside to class.

No.

She rushed forward and saw the cause: a flat tire.

She looked back across the empty parking lot to the building. All the windows were dark. Her professor had likely gone out to the staff parking area on the far side. He was probably long gone. *Crap.*

She could call her father, but it would take him an hour to get here, maybe more in this weather.

She could change a tire. Probably. Besides, what choice did she have?

After stowing her backpack in the backseat, she went to the trunk and lugged out the spare. It took some doing to find the jack and tire iron in the dark and swirling snow, but she managed it.

She was sure she'd ruined her jeans in the parking lot grime, but she cranked the jack and got the car lifted. Her hands were numb. She blew on them in a futile attempt to warm them, then gripped the icy tire iron and slid it over the nut. She yanked and pulled, but that nut wouldn't budge. She tried another bolt with the same results.

Her lungs constricted in the cold air.

How long could she sit in the running car before she ran out of gas? Was she even supposed to be in the car with it up on the jack like that? She stared, shivered, and told herself she was not going to be the first student at this campus to die of a flat tire.

And then a pair of headlights sliced through the night and falling snow. A car door slammed, and a familiar voice called out. "You having trouble?"

Justin.

Relief brought hot tears to her eyes, but she didn't dare let them spill, not with her lashes already clumped together with snowflakes.

"Just a flat," she said, trying to keep her voice even.

"Let me take a look."

He brushed past her, his gait just slightly off. She worried about that leg, remembering those videos of him being stepped on. Her hand flashed out and she clasped his forearm. "Wait."

He stopped abreast of her, their shoulders almost touching. His hat shielded his face from the snow and kept his eyes in shadow.

"I don't want you to hurt yourself."

He shifted and looked at her. She couldn't read his eyes, but his jaw tightened perceptibly. There was a dangerous tone in his voice when he said, "What do you mean?"

"Your injury—can you lift…?"

He jerked away, giving her his back. "It was my pelvis, not my back."

He bent over the jack, turned, and picked up the spare tire. He squeezed it between his hands. "You've got a problem here. Your spare is flat too."

"It is?" Doom.

"Yep."

His voice was so matter-of-fact, while tears stung her eyes. She fumbled in her pocket, attempting to pull out her cell phone. "I can call my dad."

He knelt beside her car and lowered the jack. Probably wise if it had to be left out here overnight. "Shops are going to be closed. I'll drive you home."

He didn't leave her room to argue. She was so cold… nearly numb. Her teeth chattered as she said, "I need my b-b-b-backpack."

He grunted an acknowledgement. "Get in the truck."

She trudged through the already-deep snow and fumbled with the door handle, her hands stiff and knuckles not working. Then he was behind her, his gloved hand closing over hers on the handle, popping the door open, then boosting her inside.

He had left the engine running and just being out of the wind was a relief, but it wasn't as warm as she'd expected.

She let her eyes close, exhaustion seeping over her.

Moments later, there was a rush of cold air, and then the driver's side door shut with a thud. Something big hit the bench seat between them. Her backpack.

"Where are your gloves? Are you falling asleep? You might be hypothermic."

He sounded angry. There was motion on his side of the truck, the sound of cloth rasping, like maybe he'd taken off his gloves.

"I wasn't r-r-r-eady for the cold," she said, as if that weren't obvious.

He reached for her, chafing her hands between his larger ones. "The truck's heater is on the fritz. It works, but not very well."

"It—s ok-kay," she said through chattering teeth. "Thanks for stopping to help me."

He said something under his breath, and his eyes were still burning when he looked at her.

"You rush into class without eating supper. You don't have gloves on one of the coldest nights of the year... You need someone to take care of you."

His words were like a blast of arctic air across her face. She snatched her hands back, glaring up at him. "I can take care of myself."

He ignored her, nudging her backpack onto the floor. He wrapped one strong arm around her waist and tugged her across into the middle of the bench seat.

"What are you doing?" she squealed, struggling ineffectively.

"I told you, the heater is on the fritz. I'll have to warm you up."

He tucked her under his arm.

And it *was* warm.

I can take care of myself.

Valri's words reverberated in Justin's brain as he peered through the swirling snow. Visibility sucked. He was going twenty on a state highway, afraid to go any faster for fear of running off the road. The snow had started to pack into ice. His tires skidded and his hands flexed on the wheel as he carefully guided the truck out of it.

He was having more than a little trouble concentrating on the slick road conditions with Valri pressed up close to his side. He'd had to let go of her, because he needed both hands to steer, but he was gratified that she had stayed in the seat next to him.

He might've offended her. She hadn't spoken since he'd pulled out of the university parking lot. Either that or she was frightened and wanted to let him concentrate on driving. Once she'd warmed up some, she'd pulled out her cell phone and sent off several text messages, her phone buzzing multiple times and letting off a blue glow in the dark cab of the truck.

The silence was starting to make him uncomfortable. He'd had a meeting with his faculty advisor earlier in the afternoon and parked in a secondary commuter lot. When the Comm 2 prof had dismissed class, Justin had cleared out with the rest of the students.

But after the long walk in the freezing, blowing snow, something inside had urged him to drive through the other parking lot.

He didn't want to think about the paralyzing fear he'd felt when his headlights had cut through the snow and illuminated her standing near her car. What would she have done if he hadn't driven by? Probably called Daddy, but she'd been out in the cold long enough that she wasn't firing on all synapses when he'd put her in his truck. There was a chance something worse could have happened to her—like hypothermia.

And that didn't bear thinking about.

Nor did he want to think about her *concern* when she'd asked if he would be okay to change a tire. As if he were an invalid because of a little limp. His ego had taken a definite hit.

He didn't want to think. Period.

"Why do you want to be a doctor so badly?"

He ground his teeth after the question had already popped out. It was too personal, and the last thing he needed was to get personal with her.

"When I was eight, one of my younger brothers fell off his bike and busted his face. I'm not talking scrapes and bruises— he had to have twenty stitches and get his broken nose reset."

Ouch. He'd broken his nose once on the back of a bull. It hurt.

"My parents were at work and had left my older brother Kevin in charge. There was blood all over—and Kevin is not good with blood. He was in hysterics, talking to the 9-1-1 operator, and somehow, I just knew what to do. I went to the bathroom cabinet and got some towels to staunch the bleeding. I talked to Steven, told him that he'd have a cool scar, better than any of his older brothers had, and that seemed to make him happy. When the paramedics got there, one of them looked right at me and told me I'd done a good job. That I could be a doctor one day."

It was a nice story. His childhood hadn't been roses like that, with family all around and a doting mother. His own mother had shut down after his had dad died, leaving Maddox in charge most of the time and short-wiring both of their childhoods.

"Plus, there's the money."

His eyes slid to her. He couldn't help it. He jerked his gaze back to the road quickly, but she stared straight ahead, looking as serious as all get out.

"You don't seem like the kind of person who worries a lot about money." Her clothes weren't cheap or worn, but neither were they designer labels.

"When there's never enough to stretch far enough, having a comfortable life seems like a worthy goal."

He wanted to ask more, but before he could, she tilted her head toward him. "How long were you in the hospital after that bull stepped on you?"

Everything in him clenched tight. He'd asked her a personal question, and he supposed it were only fair that she do the same. But he didn't like to talk about those days—tried not to think about them, except when he was rehashing his life story in the twelve-step program he worked.

"Long enough," he said through stiff lips. "Couple weeks by the time the surgeries were through."

And he'd been bedridden at home for months after that.

Either she'd picked up on his tension, or her mind had flitted in an entirely different direction, because next she asked, "What's your major? What are you going to do with your degree when you graduate?"

"I'm undeclared."

"It's a lot of money to spend on a piece of paper if you're not going to use it."

He laughed. "I guess it is. Haley—that's my sister-in-law—pushed me to go back to school. I think she was hoping I'll figure something out by the time my four years are up."

"What do you do when you're not taking classes?"

What was this, Twenty Questions? Or had she been storing up all this curiosity when they were in class together? He'd been trying so hard to keep his distance, maybe he hadn't noticed.

"My brother, Maddox, and I have joint ownership of a family farm. He's a high school football coach, so I do the work—grow alfalfa and manage a couple of cows, couple of horses. My brother has custody of our niece, and I try to help out with her when I can, too."

"So you're really a cowboy, even though you're not on the rodeo circuit anymore?"

He nodded and then spoke before she had a chance to ask another question. "How many jobs do you have? You're always rushing in to class like you barely have time to breathe."

And he shouldn't admit to having noticed, but there it was.

Valri took every opportunity to study Justin's profile, as he had to concentrate on the road.

She'd noticed the fine lines that had appeared around his mouth and at the corner of his eyes when she'd mentioned his injury and the hospital stay after. And how his eyes had softened when he'd talked about his sister-in-law and his niece.

But he'd turned a question back on her. "Paying jobs or everything?"

"Everything."

She started counting on her fingers. "I work at the Coffee Hut, as you know. I also fill in at my dad's hardware store, volunteer at the free clinic, and help take care of my brothers and sisters. And I'm a student."

"That's a lot of responsibility."

She shrugged. She hadn't known any different. She'd been working at her dad's store unofficially since she was twelve—all her siblings did. There was never enough money to go around, and she had big goals. She loved her mother, but she didn't want to end up like her.

"I'm trying to limit my student loans to actual med school, because I know my study load will be higher then. It makes sense to work now, before that time hits."

He glanced at her, high brows slightly furrowed. She couldn't read him. Maybe he was trying to figure her out, too.

The truck lurched and the tired locked, sending them spinning toward the ditch. Her seatbelt snagged her waist. Her heart thudded in her ears.

Justin calmly corrected their trajectory.

She didn't want to distract him, didn't want anything to make their journey more difficult.

"What are you worrying about over there?" he asked.

"Hmm?"

"I recognize the signs from sitting next to you all these weeks. You're chewing your lip and you have a little crinkle right here." He pointed to the bridge of his own nose.

She didn't want to admit that her thoughts had been centered on him. Again.

"I'm concerned about my car. I can't believe I didn't know the spare was flat."

She wasn't a *car person* per se, but she knew how to check the oil.

"One tire shouldn't set you back too much."

He said the words casually, but her budget was so tight... She hadn't even thought about the monetary implications. Maybe that was a by-product of being too cold. Not to mention the brain-fuddling that came along with riding in a truck beside Justin.

The money. She didn't want to think about it now. She'd have to do some juggling in her checkbook to pay for the repair.

"Where is your farm?" She'd given him basic directions to

her parents' house on the outskirts of Redbud Trails earlier. They'd shared a chuckle over the fact that they'd grown up in the same town, but their age difference meant they hadn't been in school together. Funny how that one connection at the Coffee Hut had turned into something more.

"Opposite side of town from you. Assuming I can get there."

"Maybe you should stay for a while. Until the snow stops, at least."

His nose was only inches from the windshield, he was leaning so far forward in an attempt to see through the snow.

The truck skidded as he turned on the street leading into her neighborhood. "I may have to. The roads are getting worse."

"Does Redbud Trails even have a snowplow?"

She felt the hum of his laugh through her shoulder, which was pressed again his upper arm.

"One, I think."

The truck crawled along her street. The snow had really drifted here, and his tires spun, searching for traction.

And then he turned into her drive, and the truck tires refused to grip at all. Her parents owned five acres, and the house was set well back from the street. Lights glowed within, an anchor in the swirling snow and dark.

"Looks like we're walking from here." He cut the engine.

"My dad and brother can come back and help you try to get unstuck."

She roused from her comfortable nest up close to his side, reaching for her backpack. "I'm sorry you had to drive me home. If my tire hadn't been flat, you could've been home by now."

He had one hand casually over the top of the steering wheel, a pose she'd seen him in often as he drove through the Coffee Hut.

But his other hand came up and tucked a strand of hair behind her ear, then the meaty part of his thumb rested against her cheek.

Heat swept through her and up into her cheeks as he stared down into her eyes.

"I'm not sorry. If your tire had blown out on your way home, you could've been stranded out in the middle of it."

His eyes flicked down to her mouth, so briefly that she might've imagined it. Because she wanted him to kiss her...?

Had his head tilted down an infinitesimal amount?

And then suddenly, he let go and popped his door open, cold swirling in and breaking the spell.

She grabbed her backpack and shrugged it on, then followed him out of the car. She sank into snow up over her ankles, and she gasped as the cold seeped down into the tops of her tennis shoes.

"You good?" Justin asked. He slammed the door closed behind her.

"Yeah. I'll be better when I'm inside." Her teeth were already chattering.

The wind whipped icy pellets against her cheeks with stinging force until they felt raw. The moisture slithered down the neck of her coat, and she wished again for a scarf.

She stumbled up the long, gravel drive, concentrating on putting one foot in front of the other.

And then Justin's arm came around her shoulders, steadying her. With his broad shoulders breaking the wind, she was slightly warmer.

"I sh-should warn you," she said, teeth still chattering.

"About what?" His voice was warm in her ear, even if his breath wasn't.

"My two older brothers are married and gone, but there are still eight of us at home."

She lost her footing, and his tight grip kept her from falling face-first into the snow.

"That's right. I know you're one of ten. But what's the warning for?"

"Just..." She half-laughed, the sound whisked away by the howling wind. "They won't leave you alone, from the moment you step inside."

She thought he chuckled, but she couldn't be sure. "I think I can handle myself."

At least he couldn't say she hadn't warned him.

CHAPTER SIX

Justin had thought that Valri was exaggerating about her siblings, but when they pushed in through the front door, four little people fell on them immediately.

He squinted in the bright lights—at least they seemed bright after being out in the elements—as a child of four or five grabbed his hand and hung on, the tyke's weight surprising him. His arm naturally flexed to catch the boy.

"All right, let them have some room!" exclaimed a boisterous male voice. Justin looked up to see a man who shared Valri's sparkling brown eyes and dark hair coming in from another room—what looked to be the kitchen.

"My dad," Valri said, disengaging from him, and Justin realized he'd still had her secured under his arm. Snow cascaded off of their coats and onto the floor.

"John North."

"Justin Michaels."

There was a glint of recognition in the other man's eyes as he squeezed Justin's hand in a bone-breaking grip, sending more snow drifting to the floor.

"Who's Justin?"

"Do you have a boyfriend?"

Little voices turned Justin's head down to the four still jostling between him and Valri. Two towheaded boys of approximately eight years old had to be twins, they looked so much alike. A girl with brown hair was in between them and the youngest, who still hung on Justin's arm, regardless of his dad's earlier order.

"He's a friend. From my Comm 2 class," Valri explained. "My car had a flat, and the spare turned out to be flat too."

Her dad's forehead wrinkled. He knew the danger of such a situation, that much was obvious. He clapped Justin on the shoulder, hard enough that Justin had to move one of his feet to keep from stumbling. "Thanks for bringing my girl home."

Justin nodded, not sure what was the right thing to say in a situation like this. He'd never met a girl's parents before. Never had a real relationship, unless you counted one-night stands. And he didn't.

It wasn't like he and Valri were dating, but being here brought a strange intimacy that disoriented him.

"Justin's truck got stuck at the end of the drive. Can you and Steven help push him out?"

"Did I hear my name?" A lanky young man, probably seventeen, wandered in from a second hallway, munching on an apple. He looked more like a basketball player than a football player, and Justin wondered how much help he'd be pushing a truck.

Steven shook hands with Justin, sizing him up with a glance.

John shot a worried look at the windows that flanked the door. "It's coming down pretty hard out there."

Uh, yeah.

"Truck's stuck pretty good," Justin said.

There had been a significant dip in the driveway, a place Justin was sure flooded in heavy rains. If he had known it was there, he would've parked on the street, but Valri hadn't warned him. "I'm not sure it's worth it to try and dig out the truck—it's snowing so hard it will fill the tracks right back up." And without chains on his tires, the roads he would need to traverse to get home would be dangerously slick, too. Maddox would have already stabled the horses and there wasn't a lot they could do for the cattle, just hope they huddled up in the three-sided building at the back of the property that would afford them some protection from the wind and snow. He didn't have any reason to put himself in danger by rushing home.

Or was he making excuses to stick close to Valri?

"I told Justin he could stay the night here," Valri said quickly.

Her dad and brother crossed their arms at nearly the same time, affecting such a similar pose that Justin nearly chuckled.

But her dad nodded. "It's the least we can do as thanks for bringing our girl home."

And yet, he had the feeling he would be watched all night. Which the old Justin would've hated, but was probably for the best. "Thanks."

"I've got to balance the month-end reports," John said. "Val, you need anything else?"

She shook her head, and her dad disappeared down a dimly-lit hallway, presumably to a home office.

Steven lounged with one shoulder against the nearest doorjamb, crunching loudly into the apple.

"Mama said we could make hot chocolate and popcorn. Valri, will you help us?" One of the twins scampered off toward the kitchen.

"C'mon," the boy attached to Justin started pulling in that direction, but Justin hung back, waiting to see where Valri would direct him.

"I guess I should've introduced everyone," she murmured, stepped closer. "That imp attached to you is Vinny, the twins are James and Eli, and this is Patti." She touched the girl's shoulder, but Patti's face was downturned.

Shy, Valri mouthed to him.

"Let me take your coat." She shrugged out of her dripping, ice-encrusted leather jacket.

He slid off his coat and gave it to her, then toed out of his boots and left them near the pile of shoes that sat to one side of the doorway.

She left her backpack at the foot of a set of stairs just off the foyer.

In his stocking feet, he followed her to the kitchen, which was blessedly warm.

The kitchen had a big butcher-block island with barstools along one side. Out-of-date appliances of avocado green matched the rooster wallpaper. An open package of bread and unscrewed jar of peanut butter had been left beside a jelly-covered butter knife on one counter, alongside a crockpot with the remains of what had probably been their supper baked onto the sides.

On the island, pieces of a solar-system model lay in disarray. At the back of the kitchen, laundry spilled from another doorway that he guessed led to the combination mudroom-laundry room.

Two teens, a boy and a girl, sat at a long picnic-style dining table in an adjacent eating area, heads down and poring over textbooks. They looked up when the younger children bustled into the room and their curious gazes landed, and stuck, on Justin.

"Hey," he said with a tip of his head.

"Samantha and Sean." Valri nodded in their direction. "A friend from university, Justin."

She sighed. "I'm sorry it's such a mess."

He shrugged, but she didn't seem to see him as she turned away. She twirled the bread bag and then tied it off, screwed the lid on the peanut butter and tossed the dirty knife in the sink. She quickly put all the PB&J ingredients away and wiped down the counter.

One of the twins rifled through a cabinet at her feet, coming up with two microwave bags of popcorn.

"Let me do that," she said before he'd even stood up, snatching the popcorn out of his hands.

She sent a wry glance over her shoulder to Justin. "He's fried one microwave," she said.

"It was *awesome*!" the other twin exclaimed.

The girl at the table, Samantha, joined the conversation. "You almost burned the kitchen down." Her gaze was on Justin, not on her brothers.

The smallest boy, Vinny, had climbed onto one of the barstools and then, as Justin watched, climbed onto the island, kicking several of the solar-system's planets off as he did so.

"Vinny," Valri warned.

"My model!" cried one of the twins.

Justin made a grab for the boy, catching him around the waist.

"Sorry," Valri muttered as she scrambled after the bouncing planets.

This was *crazy*.

Heat burned Valri's chest and face as she tried to settle her siblings.

They weren't usually so wild, but she guessed that Justin's presence had heightened the normal chaos—the twins' energy, Vinny's tendency to show off, Patti's shyness.

She scooped up Mars and returned it to the island, along with Saturn and Earth, lining up the planets neatly. "We'll finish this after the hot chocolate, James." She accompanied the words with a *don't argue with me* look.

Her brother nodded meekly, but she would be surprised if he didn't argue when it came time to actually do the work.

She nodded to Justin, who was still holding Vinny with the boy's feet about eighteen inches off the floor. "You can put him down. Vinny, if you climb again, no hot chocolate for you." She turned to Justin. "Is it too late for coffee?"

Justin's head swiveled like a ping pong ball momentarily—maybe she had run on her sentences a bit. His answer was a disbelieving expression and then a shake of his head.

She winked, scooped some grounds into the basket, and started the coffee machine gurgling and spitting.

Quickly, she grabbed the full bag of popcorn from the microwave, juggling the steaming bag, and tossed the other one in there to pop.

The kids were waiting in a line with empty bowls. As soon as she had poured Eli's portion, he grabbed a handful and stuffed it in his mouth, dropping several kernels to the floor.

"Eli," she warned.

"Sowwy," he mumbled, his mouth full.

She sent them to the table and pushed a bowl into Justin's hands, though he hadn't asked for one.

She put a pot of milk on the stove to heat and started running hot water into the crockpot with dish soap. After she'd dispersed the second bag of popcorn, she poured Justin a mug of coffee. Their fingers touched when she handed it to him, and their eyes caught as well. Something almost tangible crackled in the air between them.

Until James and Eli cooed, "*Oooh.*"

She knew she was blushing as she turned back to the kitchen. She scrubbed out the crockpot, listening to the voices behind her.

"So do you like my sister?" Samantha asked.

Valri sloshed hot water out of the crockpot and onto her shirt. It burned almost as much as her face.

"Sure," came Justin's voice, easy and calm. "She's pretty cool. For a girl."

"No…" said James with a giggle. "Do you *like* like her? Like a girlfriend?"

A cry from upstairs had her sighing. The milk on the stove was just right to melt the chocolate. If she went upstairs, it would burn.

And then Justin was behind her. He touched her lower back, a reassuring brush of his hand. "What can I do?"

"Do you know how to melt chocolate?" she asked, setting a block of baking chocolate on the counter near the stove.

"Nope."

She let a small sigh escape and started to push the pan to the back of the stove. It would be ruined, and she would have to start over.

But then his hand covered her wrist. "I'll go up and get the baby if you tell me where to find it. Him. Her."

"Her. Cindy," she said, unable to suppress a smile at his fumbling.

She glanced over her shoulder and saw Samantha and Sean both had their heads bowed over their homework. She could ask them to get the toddler, but they'd probably complain and dawdle. Steven had disappeared, probably sneaking a few minutes alone in his room to call his latest girlfriend. And the longer it took before someone got Cindy out of her crib, the louder she would get.

"I'll show you," Vinny's childish voice rang out.

She gave up with a sigh.

Vinny darted back through the hall, and Justin followed, slower with his limping gait.

She heard the tread of their footsteps going up the stairs as she dropped several squares of the chocolate into the milk and watched the white streak with brown. There was a blip in two-year-old Cindy's crying, and then she got even louder.

Valri whisked the chocolate and milk together with one hand and grabbed enough mugs out of the upper cabinet with the other.

Cindy's crying increased in volume as the tread on the stairs came back down, ultimately wailing when Justin carried her into the kitchen.

She flipped off the burner as he approached and reached out her arms. They switched places naturally as he handed off the toddler. Valri brushed against his shoulder, unable to keep from noticing the muscles there.

He moved to the stove. "This ready?"

"Yes, thanks."

Cindy hiccupped against her shoulder, her cries decreasing in volume. Her little hands clutched at Valri's shoulders.

Justin carefully poured chocolate out of the pan and into the waiting mugs. Samantha came from the table to help serve the littler kids.

Valri couldn't believe Justin had seen her family like this, a little crazy and a lot loud.

But he chuckled at something Vinny said, chattering at his side. He looked up and their eyes met over Cindy's head.

His steady presence in the face of her family's chaos was a delightful surprise.

Justin sat on the couch in the family room, a pillow and

blanket spread out beside him, his hands clasped loosely between his knees. The lamps had been turned out, but the kitchen light remained on, and he knew Valri was still in there. He heard a page turn every few minutes. She was studying.

The house was finally quiet. He had thought the farmhouse he and Maddox shared was noisy, especially now with thirteen-year-old Livy rattling around making ice cream, and with the newlyweds giggling together over private jokes.

But the North family was something else. So many kids.

And Valri took it all in stride. She'd managed their snack and helped with their homework before sending them to bed. There had been a couple of skirmishes and some light complaining, but they'd gone.

She'd even settled the toddler with a cup of warm milk and a soft song that he'd overheard, and something huge and important had shifted in his chest cavity. She would be a good mom someday.

He shouldn't go back into the kitchen. He should definitely keep his distance from her, like he'd been doing during the weeks they'd sat side-by-side at school.

But without his consent, his legs had him standing up, and his feet were moving in that direction.

She glanced up from her textbook, and she looked just like he'd imagined she would. She had two textbooks open on the counter in front of her and was perched on a barstool with a notebook open and her pencil poised to continue her notes. A laptop had been pushed to the side. Its screen was dark.

Her eyes softened when she saw him, and it took everything in him to stop in the doorway. He leaned his shoulder into the doorjamb, telling himself he wouldn't get any closer to her.

He shouldn't have come this far.

She'd changed into soft pajama pants and wore a sweatshirt, and with her hair down around her shoulders and her face scrubbed clean and shiny, she looked so adorable… and so innocent.

"You okay?" she asked. "Did you find the toothbrush I left

for you?"

He had. Somewhere in the middle of wrangling all the kids, she'd set out a new, packaged toothbrush and some soap for him in the downstairs bathroom.

"I'm fine."

But he still stood there, unmoving.

"That coffee making you too jittery to sleep?"

He snorted softly, his mouth twisting in a smile. "No." He figured he'd wrecked his body badly enough with the pain pills, the caffeine barely made an impact.

Before she could ask him something else, before he could think better of it, he said, "Is it always like that?"

Her cheeks turned pink, and she ducked her head.

His feet moved without his permission, carrying him forward to the opposite side of the island. He put his hands out and gripped the cool wood surface. He wasn't going to get any closer than this. He was close enough to see her thumb run nervously over the corner pages of her textbook.

"No," she said softly. "My siblings are usually a little better behaved. I think having you here sort of… increased their normal level of orneriness. They kept trying to guess if we were more than just friends." She laughed a little, but there was a bleak, self-mocking light in her eyes.

He gripped the counter as if his life depended on it. Until his knuckles turned white.

"So… you have a full load at the university, work three jobs—"

Her head came up. "One is only volunteering," she argued softly.

"Work *three* jobs," he countered firmly, "and come home to babysit?"

She looked back down, letting her hair fall across one cheek. Hiding? "Not every night. If my dad has to bring work home, he sort of… disappears into it. But that's only when things are too busy at the store for him to do the work during business hours."

"And your mom?" He hadn't seen her at all.

"She's a nurse. Only works ten days a month, but when she does, it's double shifts. She'll be back by breakfast."

"And you're left to take care of everyone else."

She shook her head. "Everyone has to pitch in. Steven helps tote the little kids to and from school. Sam makes lunch for everyone."

"But no one makes supper for you."

Somehow his betraying feet had carried him closer to her. He was only a few feet away, standing by the corner of the island. How had that happened?

Her eyes sparked as she stood up from her barstool. "I can make my own supper," she said, a bit stiffly.

"You don't."

"I don't have *time*."

But she'd had time to sit with James and finish the solar system model, time to sing to her littlest sister, who'd woken in distress. And now she was burning the midnight oil to get her own studying done.

It made his life seem wimpy. Compared to her, he was a slacker.

She looked down again, then back up at him, and there was something vulnerable in her eyes. "I don't want you to feel sorry for me. I'm… comfortable with this life."

But was she happy?

"I don't feel sorry for you." Why had his voice gotten so husky?

And when had his sorry feet taken a step closer to her? She was within arms' reach now. *I'm going back to bed.* Too bad it didn't count if he only spoke the words in his mind.

But then somehow he'd reached for her. *Reached* for her. And she came into his arms as naturally as if she'd been dreaming of it as often as he had.

He was holding her, her head tucked beneath his chin, against his chest. They fit together like a comfortable saddle blanket beneath a well-worn saddle. He could feel her quick, panting breaths against his collarbone, her heart flying.

Goodnight, he screamed silently.

But then she tipped back her head, her lips tantalizingly close, her eyes sparking with a challenge, and asked, "What *do* you feel?"

He muttered something inarticulate and took her mouth. He kissed her with all the pent-up passion he'd stored these weeks—months, since the first time he'd seen her at the Coffee Hut.

She met him with the same intensity, melting into him. And then they broke apart, breathing hard. His fingers had tunneled into the softness of the hair at the back of her head and he had to let her go.

She settled back into his embrace, her arms around his waist and her face pressed into his neck.

What do you feel?

Too much. He wasn't good enough for her. If he made any advances toward her, she would find out soon enough.

He wasn't brave like she was, chasing after her dream. He was a coward, and so he stayed silent, just holding her.

Because this moment, here, now, was all he would have.

CHAPTER SEVEN

"Don't make me go in there," Justin begged. He'd inserted humor into the words, but he really meant them. Two thousand percent.

His sister-in-law glanced over her shoulder where she stood arm-in-arm with Maddox. Livy was arm-in-arm with Justin, slightly behind the other two.

And they were on the sidewalk right in front of North's Hardware.

He didn't know how he'd been talked into this. Shopping on Black Friday wasn't his cup of coffee. Somehow Livy had lured him out of the house with promises of fun and her secretive, Christmas-gift-hunting smile.

He'd wanted the distraction.

In the last three weeks, he'd recognized the self-defeating behaviors he'd thought he'd eradicated from his life. He'd blown off Valri after the amazing kiss they'd shared, and then he'd pushed away his family. Gone for long horseback rides in the cold Oklahoma wind. Lay in his room staring at the ceiling.

He'd managed to stay ahead of the work for his university classes, but only just.

He didn't have any goals, and any attempt at trying to come up with one kept bringing back the thing he most wanted.

Until Maddox had called him to the carpet yesterday, dragging Justin out to the barn after the Thanksgiving meal and telling him to man up and be a part of the family.

And thus, Justin was here, shopping today with Livy giggling at his antics. He *did* feel a little more alive out in the

197

fresh air.

They'd already made a circuit of the downtown shops in Redbud Trails, and a stop at the feed store his and Maddox's cousin Ryan ran with his fiancé, and now this. Livy wanted to go into the hardware store.

Where Valri worked *when her dad needed help*, and no doubt they would be busy today.

He didn't want to face her. Not when his feet tried to drag him closer, when his entire body vibrated with wanting to take her in his arms and just *hold her*.

Someone like Valri would never settle for someone like him. He knew it, and even if she didn't, he wasn't going to stick around until the day she realized how broken he really was inside.

"C'mon, Uncle J. I *have to have* some more Christmas lights for the barn."

Maddox shot him an inscrutable look over his shoulder, and Justin allowed himself to be dragged into the hardware store.

He braced himself even as a giant jingle bell rang cheerily over their heads as they entered.

The building had an open, industrial look with exposed ductwork. Multi-hued lights sparkled from the rafters. Christmas music blared through hidden speakers.

And he'd been inside for all of three seconds when a small human bomb hit him in the legs. Vinny, who glued himself to Justin's knees, shouting, "Justin!"

His gut locked up.

Samantha looked up from behind the register, where she tended to a customer. A line of them waited behind that one. John waved from the back corner of the building, just his head visible over the rows of shelves between them.

Steven was carting an artificial tree over his shoulder, looking like he was about to bowl them over.

This really was a family business.

Justin bumped Livy to one side, stepping awkwardly with Vinny still wrapped around his knee.

"Who's this?" Haley asked, turning around.

"Sorry—" A breathless Valri rushed up, reaching down for Vinny, who clung harder to Justin. "He got away from me."

She wore jeans and a shapeless polo shirt with a logo that was a mix of a hammer and a compass. He got it. North Hardware. The drabness of her outfit did nothing to dampen his awareness of her. He felt instantly hot all over. He swallowed and thought how badly he needed the shock of the cold air outside.

If only he could go back in time so he wouldn't have to be here right now.

She tugged at Vinny, but he clung.

Justin couldn't help notice that she didn't look at him.

She'd tried to talk to him those first couple of class times, but he'd ignored her, blatantly turning his back to talk to Brandi instead.

"He's all right," Justin said, keeping his voice low, aware of Haley and Maddox's curious gazes incinerating him.

And Valri looked up at him, walls up in those expressive brown eyes. It was as jarring as hitting the ground after being thrown from a bull's back. "Are you sure?"

He tried to grin, tried to affect a casualness he didn't feel. "As long as he lets go before we hit the checkout register."

For the first time, she seemed to realize he was with his family. She took in Livy, whose arm was still threaded through his, and then Maddox and Haley.

"Hi. I'm Valri." She stuck her hand out and accepted handshakes from both Haley and Maddox. "That little twerp is Vinny, one of my younger brothers."

Haley introduced them all, her eyes darting from him to Valri and back.

Valri smiled with tight lips. "Justin and I sit next to each other in Comm 2."

"Oh. It's nice to meet you."

"What can I help you with?"

"Christmas lights!" Livy exclaimed, oblivious to the weird tension flowing among the adults. "We need more!"

Valri laughed. "For your house?"

"For the barn," Livy said.

"The barn is already lit up brighter than an airport landing strip," Justin complained. "I can't sleep at night with the lights shining in my window."

Livy giggled, the way he'd meant her to. It was easier focusing on the little girl. Even though he couldn't erase his awareness of the woman at his side.

"This way," Valri said, motioning to Livy, who abandoned Justin to follow her through the crowded store. Vinny finally let go of Justin and ran off, disappearing around a display of ornaments.

Haley fell back to walk next to Justin. He braced himself for an interrogation and wasn't disappointed when she hissed, "You didn't tell me the cute coffee girl was in your class."

He shrugged. "So?"

She gave him a scathing look. "So... Are you going to ask her out? *Have* you asked her out?"

A muscle in his jaw ticked as he gritted his teeth.

"It's not like that," he muttered. "And keep your voice down."

Valri glanced over her shoulder at him, her eyes shadowed, and he had to wonder if she'd overheard.

She stopped in front of a display of Christmas lights. "These are the LED kind," Valri told Livy with a hint of wicked smile in his direction. "They're the brightest, clearest light you'll find."

"That's what I want," Livy declared.

He groaned.

"We'll take six boxes," said Maddox.

Justin glared at his brother.

It would be impolite to let Valri or Livy carry the armful of boxes, so he reached to take them.

And got close enough to hear Valri's stomach growl.

She met his eyes sheepishly.

"You haven't eaten." He made it a statement, slowly following Maddox and Haley to the checkout, where Samantha started scanning and bagging the boxes of lights.

"My dad ordered a pizza earlier."

He didn't miss that she hadn't answered the question.

Suddenly John was behind them, reaching out for a bone-crushing handshake.

"You didn't eat?" her pops asked.

"We've been busy," she said defensively.

John looked around. "Store's emptying out now. Steven and I can handle it. Why don't you go eat with your friends?"

"Oh, I'll just go home."

Behind the counter, Samantha's head bounced back and forth as she ran Maddox's debit card through the register.

"Maddox had better start getting those lights up before he loses the sunlight," Haley said. But Justin wasn't set at ease—that canary-eating grin on Haley's face proved she was up to something. "But we drove separate cars. Justin, why don't you take Valri to grab a bite?"

He locked eyes with Valri over the rest of their heads. With this interfering bunch, maybe it would be easier to give in.

More dangerous, because that's what he wanted to do.

"Fine," he caved.

"Fine," she parroted woodenly.

Great.

Fantastic.

The last place Valri wanted to be was at supper with Justin.

Maybe not the *last* place, but humiliation stung her face with heat as she donned her coat and followed Justin onto the cold street. Three weeks of silence—after an earth-shattering kiss. And now dinner—and not even a voluntary dinner at that.

Three weeks of uncomfortable small talk in class. He'd obviously been avoiding her, the way he'd gotten to class just seconds before it started and then engaged Brandi in conversation after class. He'd left her two options—either interrupt or be completely obvious and wait to talk to him.

She hadn't gotten up the courage to do either.

And apparently he'd quit drinking coffee, too, at least on

the days she worked—which was almost all of them.

Well, she certainly wasn't going to throw herself at him. She didn't have time to date, anyway.

She was just confused. Because he continued to bring her supper, leaving her sandwiches, fruit, and bowls of soup on her desk. It was a kindness, one he didn't have to do. He barely spoke to her, but he provided for her... It was too much to wrap her head around.

And then this. Going to supper.

She wasn't even dressed, not unless you counted her crappiest pair of jeans and this ugly golf shirt.

Soft, light snow was falling, and the sun was setting as she walked silently beside him. Street lamps had been lit, and the huge tree outside of City Hall was strung with lights. It looked like Christmas, even if it felt more like an execution.

"Remind me to check your tires before I head home," he said, slanting a smile at her like everything was normal.

She gave a soft huff, but nothing else. She'd seen the way his eyes had cut away when his sister-in-law had suggested they go to dinner together. He didn't want to be here, even if he pretended otherwise.

He held the door open to the small mom-and-pop café, and she ducked inside before he could confuse her more by placing that rogue hand on her back. It was pathetic that she could remember so well how it felt to be tucked under his arm.

Inside, the place was packed with holiday diners, and Valri felt conspicuous—maybe more so because she knew her *date* didn't want to be here.

She turned to him and lifted her chin. "I'm perfectly capable of feeding myself. I don't need you to stay."

He nodded to a space beyond her. "There's a booth open in the back."

"I said—"

"I heard what you said." His eyes met hers for the first time since he'd come into her dad's store. There was a spark of vulnerability or desperation or bleakness in the blue depths that made her breath catch in her chest.

He took her elbow in his big hand and ushered her forward, winding through the tables.

Just that one glimpse inside of him, and she followed like a lamb.

A stupid, stupid lamb.

She slid into the booth and crossed her arms. Fine, she was here, but she refused to enjoy it. Otherwise, she'd enjoy it too much, and then where would she be? Confused again.

He surprised her by sitting next to her.

She opened her mouth to say something—*what* she didn't know—but her mind stalled out at the press of his thigh against hers. And then, before she could speak through suddenly-parched lips, the waitress was there at his elbow.

He requested coffee for himself, and she ordered a chicken pot pie.

And then they were alone again. "Why did you come into the store?"

"I shouldn't have." He looked at his hands, which were folded on the table in front of him. "I have a hard time saying no to Livy."

She frowned, the sting of his words hitting home.

And then as she traced a pattern in the worn tabletop, his hand moved to cover hers in a gentle clasp.

"I like you," he said. His voice was serious and low. "More than I should."

Joy whirled through her in a rush.

"But I don't think we should pursue a dating relationship."

And there was the bucket of icy water being poured that doused it.

She jerked her hand out from beneath his, instantly feeling the loss of the contact. She edged into the furthest corner of the booth, putting as much distance between them as she could manage.

He sighed, then fanned his fingers through his hair.

"I guess the next thing you'll say is *it's not you, it's me*," she said, voice shaky. What was she doing here? Hadn't he already broken her heart once? Here, have another shot at it, why don't you?

"It *is* me."

She refused to cry. *Refused.* It wasn't as if they had known each other very long. Only a few weeks, if she were really counting.

"You've got your big goals, you've got so much drive, and—"

"That sounds like a *me* reason," she forced out.

"And I can't even see where I'm going. I'm undeclared. Unemployed—I work the family farm part-time, but that doesn't really count." He coughed. "You need... you need to be with someone who can support you, who can be what you need him to be."

She had been shaking all over. And just like that, the shaking stopped. "I wasn't proposing marriage," she said, her voice getting firmer. "And those sound like excuses to me."

He looked up sharply at her, his eyes flashing, but she didn't miss the pinprick of fear in their depths.

"You're scared of something," she said. "Whether it's letting me in or something else..."

His eyes cut away, and she knew she was on to something. She got a tingling feeling deep in her stomach the same way she did when she figured out a medical issue in one of the patients at the free clinic, when symptoms started falling into place and a diagnosis was close.

The waitress interrupted, depositing Valri's pot pie and Justin's mug of coffee. She smiled and left, oblivious to the tension that simmered between them.

Valri opened her mouth, ready to push him for answers, but something outside herself screamed *stop!*

And she stopped. Watched him.

He brought his mug to his lips and sipped. She didn't miss the slight tremble in his hands.

Whether she'd hit a nerve with her accusation or he simply didn't like conflict, she didn't know.

But that feeling that she should stop pushing remained, settling deep inside her.

She used her fork to break the crust of her pot pie and changed the subject. "Are you going to do the extra credit for speech class?"

His expression revealed a hint of surprise as he set his mug on the table with a clack. "I don't know. I did all right on the first two presentations, and I don't have to pull an A like you're determined to. Are you doing it?"

"Yes." She had to bring her grade up. But she could only imagine humiliating herself at the improv club in Oklahoma City that the professor had revealed as their extra credit assignment. She couldn't get through a prepared speech in class, so how would she make it through several minutes of improvisation?

She ate quickly as uncomfortable silence descended on the table. She didn't know what to say to him, how to get him to open up. Or if she should.

She had no answers, and she was exhausted from a long day working with her family. The store had opened at six, and since then, she'd had a thirty-minute lunch and *this*, which was not as relaxing as one might think. She was running on fumes.

So after he'd taken care of the check and stood, she slipped out of the booth and rose to her tiptoes to buss his cheek with a kiss. "Thanks for feeding me. I'll see you next week."

Only a week and a half of class remained before their final presentation. Ten days to find a way to convince the stubborn cowboy to take a chance on her.

It wasn't going to happen.

But she couldn't just give up.

She was stubborn, too.

You're scared of something.

Justin sat on the tailgate of his pickup in the barnyard, his booted feet dangling aimlessly and his head tipped back. The snow had cleared off, leaving the sky bright with stars. He'd meant to look at them but was distracted by the garish lights covering just about every square inch of the barn.

He'd bet you could see it from space.

Tonight he really missed the oblivion that a hit of strong pain meds would give him. It wouldn't knock him out, but it would take away the edge that felt like a knife just beneath his skin. It would make him not care about the sparkle of tears that Valri had been unable to hide when they'd been at the restaurant.

Was she right?

The screen door *snicked* closed. He glanced toward the porch but after being exposed to the bright lights of the barn, his vision was spotted, and he couldn't make out who it was. Maddox or Haley. It was past Livy's bedtime.

Feet crunched on the gravel, and a soft voice greeted him. "Hey." Haley.

"Hey." He blinked a few times until his vision cleared. She stood next to the tailgate wearing what looked like Maddox's coat, her arms wrapped around her middle.

"You okay?"

"Sure," he said, as easily as he could manage. He hoped it was dark enough that she couldn't see his face, but he suspected that with the amount of glowing lights, he was done for.

"You've been out here awhile."

And he'd driven around for at least an hour after he'd walked Valri back to her dad's shop.

He had no answer for the emotional turmoil surging through him.

"Just thinking." He leaned back on his palms and turned his face up to the sky.

Maybe she would take the hint and go back inside.

Of course, this was Haley. When she'd come back into Maddox's life last year, she'd challenged Justin to dig himself out of the mire of depression and drug-induced listlessness that he'd been caught in.

She might be the only person on the planet more stubborn than he was. And he couldn't remember her ever taking a hint.

"I'm sorry if pushing you to go out with Valri re-opened some old wounds."

It hadn't. The wounds had never scabbed over.

"She seems nice," Haley offered tentatively when he didn't respond. "She seemed like someone who'd be a good match for you."

He snorted his derision. "Do you know me at all?"

"You like her." Haley didn't sound surprised. "What's the big deal?"

"The big deal is I'm no good for her. I'll keep my distance until the end of this class, and we'll go our separate ways."

"You think you're protecting her."

He jumped off the tailgate, his boots crunching in the gravel. He'd had enough of Haley's psycho-analyzing for one night.

But his sister-in-law caught his forearm with her hand. He wanted to jerk away from her comforting touch, but stopped himself. She'd been nothing but a friend to him, even those few times when he'd been in withdrawals and bit her head off. She didn't deserve his rudeness, even though that was his gut reaction.

"What are you so afraid of?"

Afraid. It was the same word Valri had used. *Was* he afraid?

"If she knew about my past..."—he barely grated the words out—"...about the meds, about the depression, she wouldn't be interested. Her family is clean cut. Nice. She's nice."

Haley held his gaze, maybe waiting for him to say more. Finally, he had to look away.

"How do you know what she'll think if you don't tell her?" Haley asked softly.

He swallowed back the words that wanted to escape. *What if it happens again? What if I'm too weak—and I ruin her life?*

He pulled away from Haley's sisterly touch, too much a coward to speak the deep-seated fear, too raw to stick around for her useless encouragement.

He stalked to the brightly-lit barn and pulled open the heavy door. Maybe throwing pitchforks of dirty hay would exhaust him enough that he could sleep.

Doubtful.

Nothing could ease the choking fear, except the knowledge that Valri was safe from him.

CHAPTER EIGHT

Valri trembled from head to foot as she stood at the back of the comedy club in Oklahoma City. The extra hour and a half drive beyond campus hadn't helped her nervousness at all.

Only a few of the students taking the class had shown up for the extra-credit assignment, along with their professor, who was handling the mic between students. Less than half the class had needed the extra credit. A few losers like her, and a few nerds who wanted a perfect grade.

She didn't have any note cards this time. No notes in improv. When she took the stage, the professor would give her a topic. And she had to find something funny to say about it. For three minutes.

She was nauseously nervous, but she was determined to do this. She had to ace this class. And who cared what her classmates thought about her anyway? Who cared what the scattered crowd thought?

All that mattered was what the professor thought.

And then she was out of time to over-analyze, because the professor was saying *her name*. And that her topic was *dating*.

She had no funny stories about dating. Only depressing ones.

She walked toward the front of the room on wooden legs. As she was passing a small alcove, she saw Justin standing in the shadows, his hands in his pockets. What was he doing here? He didn't need the extra credit.

He held her gaze, nodding to her without cracking a smile.

And suddenly she knew exactly what she was going to talk

about.

She took a deep breath and spoke into the microphone. "Good evening." The stupid thing squealed, and she stepped back and winced. The lights were so bright and the rest of the room so dark that she couldn't see anything except vague, shadowy outlines of a few people in the front rows of tables and chairs.

She adjusted her position in front of the mic and cleared her throat. "H-hello. I'm Valri."

There was dead silence in the crowd.

Three minutes, she chanted in her mind. She just had to get through three minutes. It was an eternity.

"As women, we've all heard some pretty lame reasons why guys didn't want to enter a dating relationship: From, *I'm being deported* to *My goldfish doesn't like you.* So… I thought I would talk about the top five excuses that guys give women when they're *not that into you.*"

There was a ripple of a murmur from the crowd. She didn't know if that was a good sign or not.

"So here we go. The top five reasons guys give. Number five: *I'm not looking for a serious relationship.* What does *that* really mean? Your twenty-six text messages the night after the first date might have scared him off."

There was a surprised bark of laughter from the back of the room. She squinted but couldn't see anything with the light shining in her eyes.

She took a deep breath, mind spinning ahead.

"Number four: *I don't want to be exclusive.* Translation: You're hot, but not quite hot enough for me to give up the rest of the girls I think are hot, but not quite hot enough."

Another wave of chuckles passed through the room.

She took a deep breath. She was really doing this. Her nervousness began to dissipate, and some of the shakiness left her hands.

She dared to reach up and touch the microphone as she got rolling.

"Lame excuse number three: *I'd have to change my Facebook*

status. The truth? I don't want anyone to know we're dating. On the other hand, it could be you're dating a guy who hasn't quite figured out how to change his Facebook status. And if the guy can't figure out Facebook, deal with it, honey, you dodged a bullet."

That one seemed to fall flat, meeting only silence from the room. She cleared her throat and went on.

"Number two: *We have such a great friendship I don't want to ruin it.* Ah, being relegated to 'buddy' land." She made air quotes as she spoke. "You know buddy-land, right? That's where you get the privilege of answering his middle-of-the-night phone calls because the bimbo he dumped you for smashed his truck's headlights. Can't you just hear him? 'I just told her I wanted to be friends. How'd I know she was picking out her wedding gown?' And why do guys always do that, run away like little girls? 'Cause they're scared...'"

A ripple of murmurs and laughter spread through the crowd, but she stalled out.

She hadn't meant to say that bit about being scared. She'd intended to tease Justin, not to poke his wounds. And she certainly hadn't wanted to reveal how much she cared.

Her voice trembled as she continued. "And the number one reason he'll give why he's not that into you... *I've got commitment issues.* Sounds about right. Sure, I can cheer on my losing football team for forty years, I can drink the same brand of cola until the second coming, and let's face it, I'd have to be some sort of committed to still be wearing jeans that haven't been popular since the last millennia, but when it comes to you, sweetheart, I've got commitment issues."

Something shifted inside her, as she forced out the words. A thought that hadn't crystallized until that last punch line. *Maybe he's just happy with his life the way it is.* And there was no place for her in it.

She stepped away from the mic amid laughter that rang hollow in her ears.

Justin stood in the shadows while the audience applauded

Valri's performance, his heart hammering.

I'm in love with her.

It was a heck of a time to realize that. He'd driven down in his truck, separate from the students who'd been carted down in a campus van. He'd come with some wild idea of supporting her, being here for her, even if she didn't need him or want him here. And maybe he'd lied to himself the whole time, needing to be here for *him*.

Seeing her lay it all on the line, facing her fears on the stage, highlighted once again how different she was from him. She had ambition, she chased her dreams, and she wasn't afraid to face the hard things. For her, the hard thing was public speaking, and she'd aced this assignment.

He was proud of her, even if she had been poking fun at him, trying to make light of a situation that obviously hurt, judging by the catch in her voice.

There was no way to make things right, not now, not after what he'd kept from her.

But the urgency that clenched his stomach like a giant fist forced him forward on wooden legs.

When she would've brushed past his partially-hidden spot in the alcove, he caught her arm. He opened his mouth to tell her... what? That he was sorry? That he was an idiot?

"I can't do this right now, Justin," she whispered. Her eyes were downcast, but he saw the tremble in her bottom lip.

"Don't leave," he begged. His voice was shaking as he said it.

And that earned him a look. Her eyes passed over his face, probably noting the fatigue that came from the past several sleepless nights. Her eyes softened for an infinitesimal moment before she closed her lips tightly and glared at him.

"Ssh," someone hissed from a nearby chair.

He jerked his head toward the club entrance.

She hesitated but finally nodded and followed him through the maze of tables and out into the cold air in the parking lot.

He faced her, looking down on her bent head. He didn't know if he could force words past the sick in his stomach.

He expelled a hard breath, which fogged between them. "I had thought of going up on stage and spilling everything— everything that I want to tell you. But what I have to say isn't funny."

Her gaze lifted to his face, and he shifted his feet, unable to look directly at her. He focused on a darkened building across the street. Made his throat work, when speaking was the last thing he wanted to do.

"People used to call me a risk taker. It was the nature of the occupation. But I've been a coward compared to you. You're chasing your dreams. Taking risks, like getting up on that stage."

He stared at the sky, trying to find the words to make her understand. "I thought I'd play football, like my brother, but when I was a teenager, I competed in doubles roping and then got on the back of a bull as a dare. I was good at it. Rodeo was never my plan—I just sort of stumbled into it."

He could still remember those first exhilarating rides, when it had still been fun, not a demanding career.

"It was... nice to have something for myself, to not be in Maddox's shadow. He was always the golden boy." Pushed up on that pedestal by their mother. And then Mom had died, and Justin had never had the opportunity to earn a place of his own. "And... we didn't have the easiest time of it when I was a kid. When I started having success in the arena, everything was different. I took all of it—everything that was offered to me."

He waited for her to get what he wasn't saying.

Her brow wrinkled. "Fame?"

"Women."

He saw the light dawn in her eyes. She was beginning to understand. Too bad his womanizing wasn't the worst of it. He returned his focus to the building across the street.

"At seventeen, nineteen, twenty-one... I soaked up the attention. For years, I lived my life like that. Taking what was offered with no thought for the consequences."

He wished she'd say something, anything. She was completely silent.

He felt like he was going to lose his lunch. Here came the big reveal.

"You already know how my career ended. But you don't know that after I got out of the hospital, I was addicted to pain pills. I wasted my days in fleeting moments of induced bliss interspersed with long periods of depression. My behavior hurting my family and killing me, but I didn't know how to stop. And all those so-called friends I'd made in the circuit? Gone."

He dared a look at her and saw tears had clumped her eyelashes together. His gut kicked hard.

"And now?" she asked.

"I'm clean. When Haley came back into Maddox's life, she saw what I was doing and gave me the kick in the pants I needed. But I'm still..." He shrugged, his hands fisted at his sides. "...floundering."

And that's why she deserved so much more than he could ever be.

He inhaled a deep breath and met her eyes. She stared at him, and he couldn't find words to tell her what that kiss—and her friendship—had meant to him.

And then the noisy group of university students exited the club. They must've finished up while he was unloading his heart.

He stepped away from her, and she was swallowed up in the crowd loading into the bus.

He stood in the cold for a long time afterward, hands in his pockets, staring at the corner where the taillights had disappeared. She hadn't said a word.

And maybe that's what he deserved.

CHAPTER NINE

One week before Christmas, Valri turned her Honda onto a bumpy dirt road outside of Redbud Trails.

She was really going to do this. Tell Justin how she felt.

She hadn't seen him since that night outside the comedy club.

At the time, she'd been relieved for the interruption when their classmates had exited the club. She hadn't known what to say to him then. She'd needed time to think.

And then during the last week of class, a nasty stomach virus had rampaged over the school, knocking out many students and their professor, who had cancelled classes. After that, they'd had an assigned makeup time to present their final presentation to the professor and about ten other students. She hadn't seen Justin at the presentation. Likely he'd had a different time assigned.

One of her dad's seasonal employees had quit and left the store without the needed help, and she'd had to adjust her schedule at the Coffee Hut, working odd hours. Justin hadn't come through for coffee. She'd hoped... but maybe he was still avoiding her.

She didn't have his number, but when she'd confided in her parents, her dad had mentioned driving past a huge barn lit up like something from a Chevy Chase movie, and she'd known what she had to do.

She'd spent the afternoon at the free clinic and still wore her scrubs beneath her winter coat. Twilight fell around her as she guided her car over the rutted road. And then she saw it.

The garish lights were already visible, the entire roof of the barn had been covered and crisscrossed with white and multi-colored lights. The lines of the building, each corner and the high windows, were lined with red and green. And two trees flanking the building had been wound with blue ones.

It *was* bright. And made her smile, thinking of Justin's niece and her excitement. She knew his complaints about the barn were in jest. He'd said he loved Christmas that first night of class during introductions.

Her heart in her throat, she pulled her car over the cattle guard and up a well-tended gravel drive. Justin's truck was parked next to a white, two-story farmhouse. She parked next to it.

She was met by a huge black dog with a lolling tongue. It didn't look *that* dangerous, so she stepped out.

She closed her car door and turned at movement near the barn. And there was Justin, just stepping out of the overly-lit place. He was wearing his Stetson pulled low, a jean jacket, and his familiar boots. He held a pitchfork like a walking stick, then stopped it in the ground when he saw her.

Stark surprise crossed his face, quickly hidden. He leaned the pitchfork against the side of the barn and came toward her. As she rounded the car to meet him, his boots crunched in the gravel, and he slid a pair of leather gloves from his hands, stuffing them into his back pockets.

"Hey." He smiled, but his eyes were hooded.

"Hi. A little late to be working, isn't it?" Now that she was here, nerves gripped her, making her fumble for words.

"You're one to talk," he said, nodding to her, no doubt noticing her scrubs. "What's going on?"

"Well, I…" *Missed you. Need you.* "I thought I saw you on campus when I was there yesterday. Near the administration building."

He nodded, scraping one hand across his jaw, and rocking back on his heels. Was he as nervous as she was?

He reached into an inside his jacket, pulled out a sheet of paper folded into fourths, and handed it to her.

It was worn, as if he'd already handled it several times.

He cleared his throat. "I declared my major."

Her head came up as she unfolded the sheet and saw it was a page printed from the university course catalog. Across the top, in bold letters, was emblazoned, "*Veterinary Sciences*."

She smiled up at him, and for the first time, noticed that something had settled deep in his eyes. He seemed more at peace.

She vaguely registered a sound like the slap of a screen door in the periphery of her senses, but she was caught in the magnetism of Justin's eyes.

"Uncle Justin, who's here?" a young voice called out.

She had to break their gaze when a small torpedo launched between them. Justin caught Livy with an arm around her shoulders. "It's Valri, my friend from university, remember?"

"Hi!" Livy was so wired, she was bouncing on her toes.

"I was just telling Valri about my major." His words were for Livy, but his eyes remained on Valri. "That I decided it was time to start taking risks again."

She swallowed against the lump rising in her throat, because wasn't that what he'd done at the comedy club when he'd told her about his history?

"I'm glad," she whispered.

Justin watched the play of emotions cross Valri's expressive face. His heart was pounding, his adrenaline pumping like he was back in the arena challenging a bull.

Valri was *here*. She'd come to him.

He'd had next to no hope of seeing her again after classes had been cancelled and their final rearranged. But she was here now.

"Don't you have somewhere to be, squirt?" he asked Livy at his side, ruffling her hair.

"No." The girl looked up at them guilelessly, the picture of innocence. She couldn't know she was intruding.

"It's okay." Valri handed him back his paper.

His stomach did a slow flip. She wasn't leaving already, was she?

"I actually came with a Christmas gift for your uncle."

She had?

She reached into her coat pocket and pulled out a small clump of greenery, wrapped with a red ribbon. He took it from her outstretched hand, realizing on closer inspection that it was a swag of mistletoe.

His eyes jerked to her face. The sun had long since set, but with the barn lit up like a runway behind him, he could see how rosy her cheeks had gone.

"What is it, Uncle J?"

Livy tried to peer up from beneath his elbow. He'd almost forgotten she was there. He put a hand on her shoulder and gave her a shove toward the house. "I'll give you twenty bucks to disappear right this second."

Livy took off running.

Valri's lips twitched, but he also saw the nervous jerk of her hands by her sides.

The sudden confidence that her gift had given him pulsed through him with each breath.

The screen door slammed behind Livy, leaving them alone in the barn-lit yard.

He stepped closer, reaching for her. She came willingly into his embrace. He let his left arm come around her waist as he held up the mistletoe so they were both looking at it.

"This is the gift?"

"Part of it," she whispered.

He tucked the sprig of leaves and berries into his coat pocket and let his hand come up to cup her cheek. His head tilted toward her—there was nothing holding him back this time—but just before their lips would've touched, he hesitated.

"Are you sure?" he whispered.

To answer, she lifted on her tiptoes to meet his kiss. She tasted like coffee and mint, a Christmas combination. One of her arms slid around his neck, the other around his waist.

And he was home.

He didn't let things get carried away, soon tucking her head against his chest, even as he placed a kiss against her temple.

"Merry Christmas to me," he murmured.

She laughed, and the sound vibrated through him from his head to his boots. Or maybe that was the joy washing through him.

"There's one more thing," she said, pushing slightly against his chest, tilting her head so he could see her face. "I'm falling in love with you."

There was only one answer to that. He kissed her again, passionately, endlessly, until they were both panting and out of breath.

"That's good," he said when he could finally speak. "Because I'm already there." He swallowed back the fear that threatened to choke him and said, "I love you."

She threw her arms around his neck, and they held each other, breathing together, basking in the joy of the moment.

"You sure I'm not too young for you?" she asked, a teasing lilt to her voice.

"You're probably more mature than I am," he returned.

"Probably?"

He laughed. If she could accept him, scars and all, he could accept the age difference between them.

"I'm glad you came out tonight." He spoke into the hair just above her ear. "Two more days without seeing you, and I was going to put my plan into place."

"What plan?" she asked, her breath hot on his shoulder.

"I told you I was going to start taking risks… I had this plan to park my truck in the drive-up window at the Coffee Hut until you decided to talk to me."

She hummed, and the soft noise reverberated through his chest. "I had to cut my hours there to help out at my dad's store. What were you going to ask me?"

"I was going to declare my love for you." Ha. The words were easier to say the second time around. "And ask if you could fit a washed-up bull rider into your future plans."

He found himself holding his breath as he waited for her answer. Even though they'd said the biggies, the ILYs, neither of them had mentioned the future. Until now.

When she hesitated a moment too long, he went on. "About my major… being a vet tech or even a vet someday is a job that's in demand no matter where I end up. So if… the woman I eventually marry ends up in Texas or Nebraska or even Alaska… I'd follow her there."

She sniffled, and he rested his palm against her jaw to tip her head back. Her eyes had filled with tears, but she was grinning. "Really?"

"Really. Somebody has to make sure you eat."

The back door burst open again, and Livy's voice called out from the porch. "Haley wants to know if you're coming inside or you're going to smooch your girlfriend some more?"

He winced. "Sorry."

Valri laughed. "You're kidding, right? When my family gets a whiff of this, it's going to be a nightmare."

He turned them toward the house, loving how naturally she fit against his side. "I think we can take them. Together."

"Together. I like that. I'll protect you and you protect me."

He nodded, grinning like a fool into her upturned face as they approached the porch steps. He squeezed her waist. "Best Christmas ever."

And it was.

ABOUT LACY WILLIAMS

USA Today bestselling author Lacy Williams grew up on a farm, which is where her love of cowboys was born. In reality, she's married to a right-brained banker (happily with three kiddos). She gets to express her love of western men by writing western romances. Her books have finaled in the RT Book Reviews Reviewers' Choice Awards (2012, 2013 & 2014), the Golden Quill and the Booksellers Best Award.

Lacy loves to hear from readers. You can drop her a note at lacyjwilliams@gmail.com or visit her website at www.lacywilliams.net.

Made in the USA
Charleston, SC
18 February 2015